PLUNDERED: A SCI-FI ALIEN WARRIOR ROMANCE

Raider Warriors of the Vandar #2

TANA STONE

Broadmoor Books

PROLOGUE

The Zagrath admiral strode onto the bridge of his battleship, his footsteps muffled by the hum of the engines and the buzz of low voices. His jaw was tight, and his hands were clasped in a death grip behind him.

"Well?" he asked his first officer, as the man with grizzled cheeks jumped to his feet.

"Nothing yet, Admiral." The officer glanced furtively at the blackness on the wide viewscreen. "Long range sensors show that nothing has approached the freighter."

Admiral Kurmog scowled at the expanse of space, as if it was the fault of the stars that the Vandar had yet to take their bait. "We are sure the human captain picked up the correct cargo?" He cocked an eyebrow. "The cargo with trackers was given to the correct freighter?"

The hint of a smile showed on the first officer's face, but he quickly suppressed it. "We are positive, Admiral. The female captain is quite distinctive, as is her dated ship."

Kurmog let out an impatient huff and dragged a hand over the smooth surface of his head and then his heavily lined brow. "I was sure the Vandar would pursue her, especially after we let it be widely known that she had called for Zagrath assistance to track down her sister even after the warlord let her ship go."

"They know she is the reason they were ambushed?"

The admiral gave a sharp nod. "The entire galaxy knows she is working with us to track down the Vandar horde as well as continuing to search on her own."

"The Vandar will not like that," the first officer said, taking his seat after the admiral lowered himself onto the sleek, high-backed chair. "They will want to punish her for her actions. We should give it more time."

Kurmog gripped the armrests as he surveyed the rest of the bridge from his elevated position. "Agreed. It has not been long since the hordes destroyed our battleship and dispersed." A muscle twitched in his jaw. "They might still be targeting the human freighter."

"The Vandar rarely miss an opportunity to seek revenge," his first officer added.

Kurmog's top lip curled. "Which is what we are counting on. Their desire to punish those who collude with us will be their downfall. As will their taking of the human female."

An uncomfortable murmur passed through the bridge officers. The thought of a human female being taken and claimed by one of the barbaric Vandar could not go unpunished.

Admiral Kurmog swept his gaze across his officers. "Do not worry. The raiders will pay for their crimes. The mercenaries we sent to the pleasure planet Jaldon may have failed, and the raiders may have stolen the female back when they boarded our battleship, but that does not mean this is over."

His first officer swiveled his head to face him. "You believe the Raas with the human will go after the freighter?"

"Perhaps not him, but there are many hordes. It took two of them to take out our battleship. Unless I have miscalculated our enemy, one of the warlords will take the bait." He drummed his fingers on the dark leather of the chair. "I have heard many of the warlords are from the same clan. They will not be able to resist."

"And once we can track a horde..."

Kurmog slapped his hand on the armrest. "We can destroy them without the brutes ever knowing that their lust for vengeance was their downfall."

The first officer chuckled low. "I wish I could see the looks on their faces."

"Do not worry. We will have the opportunity to see terror on Vandar faces soon enough."

"Admiral?" The officer tilted his head at his superior officer.

"We are done playing defense with these criminals," Kurmog growled. "Once we take out the hordes, I will make it my life's mission to find where they're hiding the rest of their species." He clenched his hands into fists. "And I will finish what our ancestors didn't have the will to do. I will destroy the Vandar once and for all."

CHAPTER ONE

Tara

I slammed my palm against the wet tile as the water trickled to a slow drip overhead. "Who do I have to screw to get a decent shower?"

As soon as the words were out of my mouth and echoing back to me in the cramped communal bathroom, I regretted them. I'd done things for much less, and I didn't want to think of what I'd had to do to keep myself and my sister alive.

Pulling the rough towel off a nearby hook, I wrapped it around my chest and stepped out of the shower stall. Not that it had done any good, I thought, as I glanced at my reflection in the warped, reflective metal bolted to the wall. Astrid was gone. After everything I'd sacrificed to keep her safe, she'd been taken captive by a ruthless warlord of the Vandar raiders.

My stomach still roiled when I thought about the day she'd left with the enormous alien. The day she'd *volunteered* to leave with him. That was what hurt the most. She hadn't been dragged off my ship, kicking and screaming. She'd walked off with her head held high.

I stared at myself in the mirrored steel, untying my hair from its topknot and letting the red curls spill down around my shoulders. Then I met my own gaze, the sea-green of my eyes the same color as my sister's and reminding me of the look she'd had when she'd said goodbye to me. She'd been determined. Determined she was doing the right thing. Determined she was saving me.

I tore my gaze away, leaning both hands against the cold basin. That was not the way it was supposed to happen. *I* was the captain of the ship. *I* was the older sister. *I* was supposed to make the sacrifices and take care of her. Not the other way around.

Since our parents had died when I was fifteen and she was twelve, it had been my job to look out for her. It wasn't that my parents had asked me to do it. Their death had been sudden and not something any of us expected. I knew I had to do it because I was the tough one, and my sister would never be able to survive on her own.

I sighed as I thought about Astrid, refusing to imagine her on the raider ship. She was timid and sensitive, a kid who'd always been more perceptive than practical. She could see into someone's soul, but she didn't have an ounce of good sense in her. Which was why she'd been a crap member of my crew, even though I'd moved her from post to post in an attempt to find something aboard my freighter that she excelled at.

It hadn't mattered to me. As frustrated as I could get with her—she was my kid sister, after all—I would never let her fend for herself. Not when I knew she couldn't.

"Why did they take you?" I whispered. It was a question I'd asked a thousand times in the weeks since she'd been gone.

I'd been willing to take the punishment for her mistake that had gotten us into trouble with the Vandar raiders in the first place. Even if it had meant dying, I was ready to do it to save my sister and save my ship. But then Astrid had gone and ruined it by begging the warlord not to kill me and to kill her instead.

Even though a part of me had never been prouder of her than I had been at that moment, I'd also been furious. She was not supposed to save me. That was my job, and one I'd done well for most of our lives. But on that horrible day, Astrid had been the one to save my life and save the ship, and she hadn't been seen since.

The ship shuddered, bringing me back to reality and reminding me that I needed to return to my post. It was almost first watch, and I always took first watch. Actually, I took most of the watches, since Astrid had vanished with the Vandar horde. Although my freighter was supposed to be delivering supplies to an outpost for the Zagrath Empire, the cargo had been taken by the raiders, and I had a new mission. I had to find Astrid and get her back—no matter what it cost.

My crew wasn't thrilled with our new mission, but so far, none of them had openly challenged me. I was the captain, after all, and I was still paying them, although our money would run out soon enough if we didn't deliver the new cargo we'd picked up for the empire.

I stepped out of the bathroom, making my way quickly down the corridor to my quarters. Luckily, the hall was empty, and the illumination was low. Most of the crew was either in their racks getting sleep, or on the bridge for the fifth watch.

I entered my quarters, edging around my narrow bed in the tight cabin. I was the only member of the crew with an actual cabin, but it was still like a tin can. The attached bathroom was so cramped that I preferred using the communal one down the hall, even though neither had enough water pressure lately for a decent shower.

"I'll get you fixed up soon," I told the ship as I thumped one hand against the wall. "As soon as we get Astrid back, I'll take you in for a full work-up."

I didn't know how I'd pay for that, of course. Once I paid the crew and got supplies, there was rarely anything left for upgrades, or even repairs beyond basic maintenance. Not that I was complaining. Not every twenty-three-year-old woman had her own ship, and I knew how lucky I was to have her.

Lucky was the right word, since I'd won the old freighter in a card game. I'd learned how to gamble from an old card sharp who liked for me to sit on his lap while he taught me. That had been all he liked and all he required, and I'd been more than happy to sit and smile and soak up his knowledge. Not all males asked for so little in return.

The tricks he taught me were the reason Astrid and I hadn't starved, and the reason my sister had never been forced to do any of the things I'd done. Even now, there were few gamblers in the sector who could match my skill. Plenty tried—the powerful aliens hated the thought of being bested by a human female—but they never won.

I pulled open an inset drawer, digging around for something clean to wear. Since our ship's water pressure wasn't working properly, that meant laundry had also been put on hold. I made a face when I realized I'd worn every item in my drawer several times already and none of them smelled clean. If we didn't find Astrid soon, we'd have to stop just because the crew would smell too ripe.

I found a navy-blue button-down and pair of pants that didn't seem too bad, shaking them both out and laying them across the foot of my bed. Opening another drawer, I let out a relieved breath. At least I still had clean underwear.

Despite the fact that I was the captain of a freighter and a deadly gambler, I had a drawer filled with lacy panties and bras. It was my one indulgence and nod to femininity. I tried not to think of the fact that many of the sets had been gifted to me by males who were grateful for my attentions. I told myself that I was using them more than they were using me, and why shouldn't I get something nice in return?

I found my favorite black bra and panties, rubbing my fingers over the sheer fabric and the delicate lace edging before putting them on. These I had bought for myself, which was probably why they were my favorites.

"Today is the day," I said out loud, even though there was no one to hear me. "Today we find Astrid."

I said these same words to myself every day, but every single day I believed them. I had to. If I thought that I would never find my sister and save her from the violent raiders, I wouldn't be able to live with myself. If I even allowed myself to imagine her on the warlord's ship for a second, fear would claw at my throat. Fear that she was being forced by that huge, tailed Vandar, who'd eyed her like she was a meal.

I shook my head again, banishing those thoughts from my brain. My baby sister was fine, and when I tracked down that horde, I would get her back and make sure nothing bad ever happened to her again. Not that I had any idea how a single junky freighter was supposed to force a Vandar horde to do anything, but I would deal with that problem when I had to.

"Captain!" The voice of my first officer crackled over the rusty comms system that fed into my room.

I pressed a panel by the door. "This is Tara. Go ahead."

Static filled the air before he spoke again. "Captain, you should come to the bridge as soon as possible."

My pulse quickened. "Have you found my sister?"

"Not exactly." More static. "More like a Vandar horde has found us."

Before I could ask him anything, the ship shook violently, sending me sprawling to the floor. *Shit. Were they firing on us?*

As I tried to pull myself up, the ship jerked and knocked me down again, my knees hitting the steel floor hard and sending pain shooting up my legs. My skin went cold as I clutched my knees. I knew what that meant. I'd experienced it before—the day Astrid was taken. I'd prayed I would never experience it again.

The Vandar had locked onto us. We were being boarded.

CHAPTER TWO

Kaalek

"Are you sure about this, Raas?"

I spun on my heel, and my leather battle kilt slapped my thighs. "I told you. Blowing that freighter out of the sky is too easy a punishment. I want to see their faces when they know they have been chased down and destroyed by the Vandar."

My *majak* scowled at me, his dark eyes narrowed and one of his black braids hung over his forehead. As my most trusted warrior and my second in command, it was his role to warn me of danger. As a warlord of the Vandar raiders, I rarely listened.

"Jorl." I clapped a hand on his bare shoulder. "We have been pursuing this sad ship all over the sector." I spread my arms open wide. "*Tvek*, we aren't even supposed to *be* in this sector."

"All the more reason to fire our torpedoes and be done with it." Jorl flicked his gaze to the wide view screen that stretched across the far end of the command deck and the battered freighter we'd disabled. "There are plenty of Zagrath ships to raid in our own sector."

I grunted, waving for him to follow me as I left the command deck. "If my elder brother had taken care of this like a Raas of the Vandar should, we would not need to be here. If he had destroyed this ship, instead of showing them mercy and taking one of their females, they would not have been able to send the Zagrath Empire after him and almost destroy his horde."

"Yes, Raas." My *majak* addressed me by my title as he followed me through the iron labyrinth that was our warbird. The lighting was dim, as Vandar preferred it, and I knew the way by heart. We leapt down flights of stairs and pounded across suspended walkways, the metal rattling beneath our thick boots.

"You do not approve of me leading this raiding mission?" I asked, sliding down the rail of a spiraling staircase.

Jorl hesitated. "I think it is unnecessary. You are Raas Kaalek of the Vandar, second son of the legendary Raas Bardon. You do not need to concern yourself with these humans."

I flinched at his description of me. Second son. No matter how many battles I won, or how many trembled at the mention of my name, I would always be the second son. I fisted my hands by my sides and stopped short. "And what do they say about me, *majak*?"

Jorl almost ran into me. "That you are the most ruthless Raas, and you win battles no one should be able to win."

I gave a sharp nod. "And do they say that because I stay on the command deck and watch others fight for me? No. They say that because I spill more Zagrath blood than any of my warriors."

"Yes, Raas."

I turned and started walking again, but my anger had burned

out. "I know you only wish to give me sound advice, Jorl, but I am leading this raiding party."

We reached the wide doors leading to the hangar bay, and he rested a hand on my arm. "You need prove nothing, Kaalek. You are Raas. There are none more elevated in our world. Not only that, you have just destroyed a Zagrath battleship and saved your brother's horde. We should be celebrating your achievement, not bothering with a worthless human freighter."

I met his eyes. If any other warrior had addressed me like that, I would have taken off their head with a single swing of my battle axe. But Jorl was my *majak*. He was the only warrior who knew me so well and could talk to me as an equal.

Jorl had been with me since before I'd taken my role as Raas. He was as loyal as he was wise, but his logical mind did not feed my need for vengeance and glory. He might have been right about our victory over the Zagrath, but he did not understand that celebration did not feed my need, either. Only the next battle and the next victory did that.

I inclined my head slightly. "You are right that our horde deserves a chance to let off some steam. After I have dealt with this irritation, we will celebrate our victories." I glanced at his hand on my arm. "But for now, we have a ship to raid."

He dropped his hand and his eyes. "Yes, Raas."

Striding into the hangar bay, I surveyed the warriors boarding the transport. Like all Vandar warriors, they were tall and broad, with only battle kilts covering their bronze skin. Dark, straight hair hung long around their shoulders, and long tails tipped with black fur twitched in anticipation of the battle.

I took long steps past them, jumping easily into the ship and turning to face them. "Are you ready to bring glory to Lokken, and the gods of old?"

They roared their assent.

I raised an arm high. "For Vandar!"

They pumped their fists in the air. "For Vandar!"

My *majak* jumped on board beside me, and I cut my eyes to him. "I thought you deemed this mission pointless."

The corner of his mouth quivered. "A raiding mission is still a raiding mission."

I threw an arm around his shoulder as the ship's ramp slammed shut, and the engines rumbled to life beneath our boots. "And battle is still battle."

We both grabbed for overhead rails to keep us steady, as the other warriors standing around us shifted and the transport shot out into space. My heart raced, and my skin prickled with excitement at the impending battle. Even though the freighter was old and outmatched, I hoped the crew was preparing for a fight. Too many of our raiding missions were over before they had even started, the Zagrath soldiers no match for our warriors, even with their blasters and shielding.

The ship jolted as it locked on to the enemy freighter. Although this freighter did not belong to the Zagrath Empire, it transported supplies for them, which made it complicit in the empire's chokehold of the galaxy. I would feel no guilt in punishing them. I tapped my fingers across the hilt of my battle axe. Actually, I would enjoy it.

When the ramp of our transport opened, I braced myself for an instant onslaught and prepared to race out of the ship with my weapon drawn. Instead, the small hangar bay of the freighter was empty. No shuttles. No soldiers. Nothing.

I clenched my jaw, trying not to be overwhelmed by the crushing disappointment. This would not be a glorious battle after all. "Strip the ship of anything we can use. Kill anyone who resists."

My warriors grunted in acknowledgment as we poured out of the transport and began moving through the freighter. As was Vandar custom, we moved as one, splitting off two at a time to explore different corridors.

Even though I carried my battle axe in front of me, there was no enemy to strike down. No one to even chase. I twisted to look back at Jorl. "Did they abandon ship before we arrived?"

"I do not think so, Raas." He swallowed. "Unless the ship was empty to begin with."

I let a low growl escape my throat. If word got out that I'd personally led a raiding mission onto an abandoned ship… I did not want to think what my brothers would say. At least my father was not alive to express his disapproval. He would have had plenty to say about my impulsive behavior and rash decisions. Not that he'd been around to say anything to me. I clenched my weapon tighter. I was glad I did not have to hear his voice—or my vague memories of his sharp tongue.

A burst of static made me stop suddenly and swing my attention to a door that looked slightly wider than the others. Without a word, Jorl twisted his leg up and kicked in the door, making it fly off the hinges and into the room.

There was a scream as I stormed inside, almost running into the only creature inside the tight space. I raised my axe then paused when I realized that it was a female standing in front of me. A human female with hair the color of fire cascading around her shoulders in waves. A human female who wore nothing but a few wisps of black fabric covering her breasts and her sex.

She'd been leaning over a tablet on a desk jutting out from the wall, but she swiped a hand across it to make it go dark. She squared her shoulders and glared at me, her expression one of challenge.

Only my *majak* stood behind me, and he did not speak as I gaped at the female. When I finally spoke, my voice was low. "Are you the only one, female?"

She nodded. "There's no one else on board. And you can call me Captain."

"Captain?" I stifled the urge to laugh. "You wish me to call you captain when you're dressed like a pleasurer?"

Her cheeks flamed as crimson as her hair. "I'm not a pleasurer. I'm the captain of this ship."

"What is your name?"

She paused before responding. "Tara."

"Tell me, Tara," I said. "Did you come on board to suck off the captain, and they then left you behind when they ran like cowards?"

Her hand darted up and slapped me hard across the face so fast I didn't even see it until her palm cracked against my cheek. Jorl sucked in a sharp breath moments before I advanced on her, pinning her against the wall.

"That," I said, my voice trembling with rage, "was a mistake."

Her body shook as I pressed against her, but her eyes burned into mine. "Not if you're the Vandar asshole who took my sister, it wasn't."

My body was so much bigger than her slender frame that I had to bend my neck uncomfortably to look down at her. "You think I am Kratos?" Another laugh threatened to bubble up in my throat. "I am not him, but I am also a Raas of the Vandar, and you should be much more afraid of me than of him."

"I'm not scared of you," she said, but her voice wavered.

I slid one hand from the hilt of my axe to the curve of her hip, slipping my finger under the strip of fabric that would have been so easy to rip off. "You should be. I am not like my brother. I have no intention of taking a human female as a mate." My gaze dropped to her chest and the rise and fall of her soft mounds. "Although you are more appealing than I would have imagined."

She attempted to push against me, but her attempts were futile. My cock swelled at the sight of her struggling, and I ran the tip of my tail up the side of her leg, savoring the softness of her skin. I had no desire to take any female as a mate, but I would not mind dominating this creature. Especially if she continued to resist as valiantly as she was now. It had been a long time since I'd had a worthwhile opponent. I ground my hard cock into her, and her eyes widened.

I let my finger trace the swell of her hip as she stopped moving but heaved in jagged breaths. "Would you prefer death, or would you prefer to be my whore?"

"Death," she spat out.

I smiled and moved my hand from her waist to her jaw, tilting her face up until her eyes met mine and our lips were so close her desperate breath feathered across my skin. Her eyes were a shade of green I'd never seen before, even though the pupils were so large the green was now a thin ring around the black. And though her chin was jutted out, it trembled in my grip. Fear. She was terrified even as she openly defied me and courted death.

"Good. That's what I hoped you'd say." I stepped back and turned away from her, flicking my gaze at my *majak*. "*Vaes*—and tie her up and bring her with us."

CHAPTER THREE

Tara

It took me a beat to realize what the Vandar raider had said, even though he'd spoken the universal tongue. I watched him walk away from me, his tail swishing behind him and his broad shoulders bumping the sides of the door as he tried to leave my quarters.

Even though I'd seen Vandar raiders before—when they'd boarded my ship and taken my sister—the Raas who'd just threatened to kill me and then ordered his warrior to take me was different than the others. For one, he wore black straps crisscrossing his chest in both directions, and leather caps shielding his shoulders like ebony scales. Leather ringed his wrists, and his belt was studded with metal. Every other Vandar I'd laid eyes on was bare-chested, except for the one who'd taken Astrid, which was why I'd thought this guy was him. That, and they both had square jaws and full lips that any woman would die for. It made sense that this Raas was the other one's brother, although I had a feeling that this warlord made the other one look like a pussycat.

He didn't glance back at me as he stomped off.

"No fucking way!" I kicked out as the other raider advanced on me.

Although he was huge and armed with an ancient-looking axe, his gaze was not predatory. As a matter of fact, he looked like he would have rather been anywhere but with me. When my heel connected with his shin, he winced. "*Tvekking* human."

"I am not going with you." I lowered myself into an attack crouch. "I don't care what that asshole said."

The Vandar who'd gotten stuck with me narrowed his eyes. "He is the Raas, and if he says you're coming, then you're coming." He swept one arm out, spinning me around before I could stop him and flattening me against the wall. He bound my hands swiftly, then jerked me around so I faced forward. "It is done. Do not ask me why."

As I was propelled out of my quarters and down the corridor, I was glad that we didn't encounter any of my crew. That meant they'd gotten my command to hide and were now stashed below the flooring panels, waiting for the Vandar to leave. One advantage to winning a freighter off a smuggler was that it was filled with hidey-holes. And not just any old hidden compartments—spaces that required codes to open or were a compartment inside a compartment.

I'd never used them before—and never had to—but no way was I going to lose another crew member to the Vandar. We'd gotten lucky the first time the Vandar had boarded us, but I suspected we wouldn't get lucky twice. As soon as the raiders had locked onto our ship, I'd given the order for everyone to hide. Unfortunately, I'd been too busy trying to lock the ship's controls to hide myself—or get dressed. As the Vandar led me toward the hangar bay, I started to regret not prioritizing pants.

When we reached the hangar bay, I swallowed hard when

I saw the Vandar transport. Even their functional vessel looked menacing, with its black hull and grasping wings stretched out to the sides of the ship's gaping belly. Bare-chested raiders rolled barrels up the ramp and carried crates in pairs.

"Why are you taking my cargo and supplies?" I yelled, forgetting for a moment that that was what the Vandar did—stripped vessels.

The Raas stood at the bottom of the ramp, his eyes tracking me as I was tugged forward and his tail swishing rapidly behind him. "What do you care? You're the only one on the ship, and you're coming with us."

I pressed my lips together. The bastard was calling my bluff. Did he know I was lying about the crew?

"It would be a shame for the supplies to go to waste," he continued. "Not when someone can use them."

My stomach clenched at the thought of my crew coming out and discovering the ship stripped of everything they'd need to survive. At least my first officer was smart. He'd know how to get to a nearby outpost and find help. If it was Zagrath, even better. The Zagrath would be eager to help a crew that had survived the Vandar.

As much as working for the Zagrath left a bad taste in my mouth, they did hate the Vandar raiders more than just about anything. Probably because the rebel warriors were the only reason the empire hadn't been able to solidify their hold on the galaxy. No matter how many colonies they attempted to press into service, the Vandar were always nipping at their heels and terrorizing their soldiers. If I didn't despise the Vandar so much for taking my sister, I might be impressed by their sheer tenacity.

The warrior holding my arms started to pull me up the ramp onto the Vandar ship, but I tugged against him, twisting my head to look at the leader. "You've taken everything of value on my ship. Why don't you leave me? I promise I'm more trouble than I'm worth."

One of his dark eyebrows twitched as he appraised me. "That might be the first truthful thing you've said to me, female." The amusement left his expression. "You should thank me for taking you. I'd think you'd want to be far away when we blow up this old ship."

My knees buckled, and the other Vandar had to catch me before I hit the floor. "What? You're going to blow up my ship?"

"Zagrath sympathizers must be punished." He tilted his head at me. "Why do you care? You were never going to see it again."

My stomach heaved, and I tasted bile in the back of my throat. I couldn't let my crew be blown up. They didn't deserve that. I thought of each member of my rag-tag crew—most of them just trying to scrape by, like me—and then I thought of them dying in a fiery explosion. No fucking way was I letting that happen. Not if there was any way I could stop it.

I jerked my arm away from the other raider's grasp and ran down the ramp so that I stood in front of the Raas. "Please," I begged, my voice cracking. "Please don't blow it up."

His gaze slid down my body, and he stepped closer to me. "What happened to the female who was willing to strike me?"

"I'm sorry about that," I said, hating the fact that I was practically groveling in front of this raider. I forced myself to meet his eyes even though his gaze was still roaming freely over my barely-dressed body.

"No, you're not." His gaze snapped to mine. "Tell me why you want me to spare this sad ship."

My breath caught in my throat. I couldn't admit that my crew was stashed throughout the floor panels of the ship. He and his warriors would drag them out and do who knew what to them. If he considered all of us Zagrath conspirators, he might feel vindicated in executing everyone.

"It saved my life."

His expression became curious, but he was silent as he stared at me.

"My sister and I had no money, and we hadn't eaten in two days. I talked my way into a high-stakes game of cards and won this ship." I looked down at my feet as the story spilled out of me, trying to forget that I was sharing this memory with a brutal raider who very well might kill my entire crew. "Astrid and I were so excited, we came on board and ate ourselves sick from the food left in the galley. This ship is the reason I didn't have to trade favors for food anymore. Since I've been captain, I've never had to do something I hated in order to survive."

"Until now." His voice was a deadly purr. "You are coming with me to survive."

"That's not my choice," I said before I could think better of it.

His black eyes flashed. "Then I will give you the choice, female. If you come with me, I will not blow up your ship."

I was confused for a moment. "Okay, but I was already coming with you."

"You were coming as my reluctant prisoner." He lowered his face to mine, whispering softly in my ear as his tail wrapped around my legs, the furry tip tickling the back of my bare thighs. "I want you to come willingly."

His hushed words sent shivers down my spine and made my pulse flutter. I hated that my body betrayed me when this Raas got close. I should feel only hatred for him. Not…this.

I drew in a breath to steady myself. "I'll do anything if you spare my ship."

"Anything?" He tangled a hand through my hair, tilting my head back and locking eyes with me. "It seems you are not as good a gambler as you once were."

CHAPTER FOUR

Kaalek

"I have done what you requested, Raas," my *majak* said as he came up behind me on the command deck.

Glancing at him, I couldn't help but notice a pink slash mark across his cheek. "She injured you?"

His face colored, masking the scratch, and he cleared his throat. "She did not like the idea of being tied to your bed."

I grunted in response, my body heating of its own accord, and turned back to look out the view screen. "I am not surprised. Her promise of coming willingly did not seem heartfelt."

Jorl stifled a laugh, as he also looked out across the warriors at their dark consoles and the wide view into space. The battered freighter floated in front of us, unmoving and seemingly dead in the water. "Will you still spare the ship?"

I flinched at the rebuke in the words. It was not common for me to spare anything, especially a ship that had betrayed a

Vandar horde to the Zagrath. But I also did not go back on my word. Even if my promise had been to a human female I now controlled. I flicked my hand at the ship. "We have stripped it of anything useful. It is nothing but a metal hull abandoned in space."

I remembered the desperation in the human's eyes when she'd begged me to spare it, and I knew it was not just an empty hull. But I had taken her deal and brought her on board, installing her in my private quarters. "Leave it. It is not worth the torpedo it would take to blow it up."

"Truly, Raas?"

I cut my gaze to my second in command. "Have I not just ordered it so?"

"Yes, Raas. As you have ordered, Raas. It is done."

My battle chief, Symdar, joined us from his attached *oblek*, although there was no prisoner in his interrogation room. He clicked his heels together and clasped his hands behind him.

Before he could ask, I told him, "The captive will not be joining you in the *oblek*."

"I did not expect her to be my prize," he said. "Not when I heard what she was wearing."

Thoughts of the female in her sheer wisps of black fabric made me growl uncontrollably, and both warriors glanced at me.

"I do not blame you, Raas." Symdar rocked back on his heels. "Some things are better than spilling blood."

"There is no guarantee blood will not be spilled, as well," Jorl added, drawing a finger down his cut cheek.

I was still not sure why I had been compelled to bring the female on board. It was not done on Vandar ships. My brother was the first Raas to have taken a human female as his war prize, and I had thought him weak for doing so. But I had also wanted what he'd taken for himself. My older brother had challenged the traditions of our people and prevailed, which meant he had still done what I had not. I curled my hands into tight fists. No matter what I did, I was always chasing my older brother.

There was one significant difference. I had no intention of taking a human for a mate like he had done. I had not even wanted to spare her, but that had been before I had seen Tara, and before she had challenged me.

Her slap had fired my blood and awakened a desire in me. She was a worthy adversary. Worthier than most I had encountered recently, and I needed to conquer her just as I would conquer any enemy who resisted me. I wanted to see the fear in her eyes again and then the submission.

That is all it is, I told myself. *A challenge. You need something to challenge you.*

And the female would certainly do that. Crossing my arms in front of me, I pushed down my swollen cock. *Tvek.* Even thinking of her made my body hum with need.

"Set a course to return to our sector," I said, turning on my heel and waving a hand dismissively at the view screen. "There is nothing left for us to do here."

Heels clicked as I strode off the command deck. There was no question in my mind where I was going, and I doubted there was any question among the warriors who watched me leave. I walked briskly through the maze of open corridors, leaping down staircases as the cold steel rattled beneath my boots. There was a comforting familiarity in the echoes and shadows of my ship, the darkness enveloping me as I descended deeper.

Pausing outside the arched door to my quarters, I pressed my hand to the side panel and waited for them to slide open. I'd expected screams or at least noises of a struggle, but it was virtually silent. The only sound was the faint crackling of an artificial fire burning in the fireplace.

Stepping inside, my gaze went to the large round bed that dominated the room with traditional Vandar battle axes crisscrossed and mounted on the wall above it. As promised, Jorl had tied the female to the straps dangling from the two top bedposts that were forged from battle-axes, the steel blades topping each post glinting in the glow from the fire. Her alabaster skin was in stark contrast to the gleaming black of the sheets, and her hair was a flaming halo around her head.

I slipped off my boots and walked silently toward her. She was not struggling and spitting venom at me because she was asleep. Her head was turned to one side and her limbs were relaxed—even the ones tied over her head. Without the determined set of her jaw and the spark in her eyes, she looked younger than I'd imagined she was.

I stood beside the bed staring down at her. It was discomfiting to see the female like this, even though she still wore barely anything. My gaze drifted from the long lashes fanned across her cheeks, and her plump, pink lips, to the swell of her breasts straining against the black fabric and the flat stomach leading to an even smaller V of fabric between her legs. I didn't bother to push down my cock, which had stiffened and tented my battle kilt, or slow the twitch of my tail as it flicked behind me. I had no one to hide my arousal from. Not even her.

I wanted to run my hands over her soft skin and see the surprise and fear when she woke up and saw me looming over her. But I also wanted to continue watching her chest rise and fall as she breathed, her eyes moving beneath their lids as she dreamed.

My only dreams were of battle and blood and being chased —and most nights I woke in a cold sweat from my violent dreams—but her lips curved upward as she dreamed. How could this human who'd lived on that sad, dilapidated freighter have anything good to dream about? I wished I could dip into her mind and know what caused the breathy sighs that made my cock ache.

Leaning over her, I lowered my head until my face almost

brushed hers, inhaling deeply the sweet, yet warm, scent of her skin. I'd never smelled anything as intoxicating in my life. I took another breath, moving my head down to her neck, my lips brushing the hollow of her throat.

Her softness was foreign to me. My world was battle axes and war cries, torpedoes and blasters. Vandar warriors were hardbodied like me, skin pulled tight over muscles that had been honed in battle. Nothing like this female with her gentle curves and unmarred skin. The need to claim her and feel her body beneath mine—her warmth sheathing my rigidness— almost brought me to my knees.

I squeezed my eyes tight, shaking my head. I could not let this female distract me. She was just that, a female brought on board to scratch an itch. Nothing more. She might be more intriguing than the pleasurers with their practiced moves and rehearsed moans, but she was only a female—and a human one, at that. I would conquer her like I conquered everything, and then I would move on.

When I realized that her breathing had changed and her sleepy sighs had disappeared, I opened my eyes. The female was no longer sleeping, but she did not seem startled to find me practically on top of her. She barely moved as her gaze took me in, her hands shifting behind her in the restraints as if she was checking to see if she was still tied up.

Then the faint smile that had been teasing her lips widened. "I've been waiting for you, Raas."

CHAPTER FIVE

Tara

I felt him before I saw him. His breath was warm on my skin, tickling me and making goose bumps prickle my flesh. But it was his scent—spicy and masculine—that made my eyes open.

I should have been terrified that the Vandar raider was almost on top of me, but his eyes were closed, and he seemed to be smelling me. This was not what I would have expected from the warrior who'd ground his cock into me as he'd pressed me against the wall of my quarters. That warrior had been intent on intimidation. This one was not even taking advantage of me being tied up or asleep. Except to smell me without me knowing.

Please don't let him have some sort of creepy fetish, I thought.

I could deal with a lot, but fetishes were not my thing. I didn't mind what any consenting adults did in the privacy of their bedroom, but I'd seen enough to know that sexual quirks weren't my jam. Nor was using actual jam—way too sticky. If the Vandar warlord was into sniffing armpits to get turned on, more power to him, but I did not want to be a part of it, thank you very much.

At least he wasn't groping me. I supposed I should have been grateful for that, although I'd be lying if I didn't admit to finding the huge alien pretty gorgeous. Aside from having an incredible body—and displaying most of it—his dark hair and eyes gave him a dangerous vibe that was like catnip for me. Not to mention the tail swishing languidly behind him, which made him seem even more the predator.

My pulse quickened as he hovered above me, but I concentrated on keeping my breath even. I was tied up tightly. The Vandar who'd been tasked with bringing me to the Raas' quarters had seen to that, although I'd made it as difficult for him as I could. When I agreed to come on board willingly, I'd never agreed to being tied up to a bed. Not that I had much say in the matter, and as long as the Vandar kept his word and did not destroy my ship, I would deal with it.

Come to think of it, as long as I was stuck on a Vandar ship, I should make the most of it. The horde warlord who'd taken me was not the one who'd taken my sister, but he knew who had her. His brother, Raas Kratos. Maybe if I played my cards right and played along with what this Vandar wanted, he would take me to her.

Faking it was no problem. I'd faked affection and desire and euphoria so often I wasn't sure what the real things felt like anymore.

When he opened his eyes and met my gaze, I gave him my most seductive smile. "I've been waiting for you, Raas."

He jerked back, standing and taking a step away from me as if my words had scalded him. "Waiting to scratch me?"

I laughed, the artificial sound high to my ears. "Only if you drive me wild with pleasure."

Crossing his arms, he frowned down at me. "You injured my

majak when he brought you to my quarters and restrained you, and now you are fine with it?"

I shrugged, experiencing a flush of satisfaction that I'd drawn blood from the warrior who'd dragged me to the bed and shackled me to the bizarre bedposts topped with what looked like round axe blades. "I've had some time to reconsider."

He waved a hand at me. "So, you do not mind this now that you've had the chance to…reconsider?"

I shook my head, wiggling my hips at him. "Not if you're here."

He turned swiftly and stomped to the door with his tail swishing, pressing a panel to the side of it. I took his distraction as an opportunity to scan the room, which looked exactly as it had when I'd been brought in—shiny, black floors with a smattering of sleek, hard furniture bolted to them. I'd been putting up way too much of a fight to notice the wall of glass that looked out into space, or the fire set into the obsidian walls. *That* had not been burning when I'd fallen asleep, and I was pretty sure the glass had been covered by a screen. Which made me wonder how long I'd been out.

A voice crackled through the panel. "Yes, Raas."

"Ask Jorl what he gave the female," the Raas said, glancing back at me and then bending lower to the panel. "What type of sedation did he give her when he brought her to my quarters? She is having a reaction to it."

I lifted my head off the pillow. Had those fuckers drugged me while I was sleeping?

There were muffled voices mixed with the sounds of static before another voice came on. "Sedation, Raas? I gave her nothing."

He twisted his head to look back at me, his eyes narrowed. "Nothing? You are sure?"

"I would never do anything like that without your permission, Raas. Even if I wanted to more than you could imagine."

The Raas grunted out a half laugh. "Understood." He pressed the panel again and let out a breath before turning.

I relaxed slightly. I didn't feel doped up, although it amused me that the Raas thought I was.

"I promise you I'm not on anything," I said, lifting my head to watch him stalk toward me. "And your warrior didn't give me a sedative. He was too busy licking his wounds."

The warlord's pupils flared. "I saw the mark you left on him." He reached the side of the bed and looked down at me, then dragged one finger up the length of my arm until he reached my fingers. "What happened to your claws?"

A shiver went through me at his touch, heat pulsing between my legs. "I guess I don't mind being tied up with you as much."

He shook his head and his dark hair swung around his face. "That is not it. You had no problem striking me on your ship. Or telling me you'd choose death rather than be my whore. Now you would spread your legs eagerly for me?"

I flinched unconsciously, and his eyebrow twitched up.

"There it is." He leaned over me, his gaze intent on my face. "That is what you really feel." He straightened. "The rest is some game you think I am foolish enough to fall for."

I sagged into the bed, my frustration mixing with exhaustion. "Fine. I'm being nice to you, so you won't change your mind and blow up my ship."

He recoiled slightly. "You think a Vandar Raas would go back on his promise?"

Was he serious? "Uh, yeah. You guys aren't exactly known as honorable."

He clenched his jaw, and I instantly regretted my words. Shit. Was this raider warlord—famous for pillaging Zagrath ships and destroying their colonies—upset that I'd accused him of being dishonest? He and his horde were probably responsible for untold damage to the empire by flying their stealth warbirds and attacking undetected, and he was mad about being called shady?

"A Raas does not lie." His words were sharp and cold. "I told you I would let your ship go, and I did. Your freighter is floating alone in space, as promised, and we are en route to my sector."

I saw no deception in his face. Then I absorbed what he'd said. "Wait. We're leaving this sector?"

He put his hands on his hips, his battle axe shifting by his leg. "That is what I said, female. My horde does not patrol this sector. It is the realm of my brother, Raas Kratos." He made a low noise in the back of his throat as he turned and walked a circle at the foot of the bed. "Not that my brother has been doing his job here like he should. But if we stay to clean up more of his mess, the Zagrath might gain a stronger foothold in my sector. I have been away too long as it is."

My heart sank. We were flying away from my sister and away from my crew. Every moment aboard this warbird meant that I was getting farther from the life I'd fought to build and being reunited with Astrid. I bit my lip to keep the tears at bay. I almost never cried, and this wasn't the time to start. "But if your brother needs your help...?"

He cut off my words quickly. "I am a Raas of the Vandar. I command my own horde. I do not serve my brother."

Okay. He clearly had some family issues and the brother angle wasn't going to work. "What happens when we get back to your sector?" I'd rarely been out of my sector, and I knew little about the others. Only that they were more lawless and less colonized.

He stopped pacing. "We do what we always do. Fight against the Zagrath to free the galaxy."

"So, you're going to go back to raiding?" I tugged at my wrists. "And what about me? Do I stay tied up here while you're busy pillaging the empire?"

He tilted his head slowly at me, then his gaze slid from my

legs all the way up to my eyes. He bent down and crawled up toward me, his knees spread so that my body was between them. Lowering his mouth, he nipped softly at my bare skin as he moved—first my thighs, then the space between my belly button and my panties, then the flat of my stomach. When he reached my breasts, he lowered his mouth to the fabric covering my nipples, sucking each one until I arched silently off the bed. Finally, he dragged his tongue between my breasts and up my neck.

Even though I wanted to close my eyes, I kept them open, forcing myself to lock my gaze on his as he held himself over me, his arms braced on each side of me and his lips almost touching mine. When he crushed his mouth to mine, I let out a small gasp. The kiss was so fast and hard and so unlike his previous caresses that all the air left me. Parting my lips, he plundered my mouth, his tongue fighting with mine. When he pulled away, we were both panting, and my wrists fell free of the restraints. I realized with some amount of shock that he'd untied me.

He got off the bed. "I don't know what I will do with you yet, but you will not be tied up. I prefer you when you can fight back, female."

Without waiting for my response, he pounded out of the room, the door shutting behind him.

I sat up, rubbing my wrists and swiping a hand across my mouth. That arrogant fucker. If he wanted a fight, I'd give him a fight.

CHAPTER SIX

Kaalek

I leaned one hand against the clear star chart that took up one wall of my strategy room. Soon, we would be back in our sector, away from the other Vandar hordes and the ship I'd left abandoned in space. None of my crew had questioned my decision to leave the ship, but that was because they knew about the female. They'd seen me take her, and it was no secret that Jorl had tied her to my bed.

I growled low. I should not have brought her on board. Not when I had scorned my own brother taking a human female. And then I went and captured her sister? It was weak—a sign that I gave in to my desires—and I was never weak. There was no room for it when I had so much to live up to and so much to prove.

I slammed my palm on the surface, and the glass rattled. There was nothing to do about it now. She was on my ship and locked in my quarters. We were far from her ship and her sector. I had nowhere to put her, even if I wished to be rid of her, which I didn't.

I might have no need for a mate, but I did find her appealing. When she wasn't simpering at me. I had no use for her sweet words and seductive looks. They were not real.

No, what I wanted was what I'd seen when I'd taken her on her ship. I wanted her fire and her fear. I wanted her so desperate and terrified that she lashed out at me. It was the only way I'd be able to conquer her and make it worth my time.

A thumping on the door made me look up. "*Vaes!*"

Symdar and Jorl entered side-by-side, their battle axes swinging and their tails swishing.

"Report," I said, knowing they would not have entered without a purpose.

They exchanged a quick glance and then Symdar spoke. "Before we left the sector to give aid to your brother's horde, we had pinpointed a new Zagrath outpost on Carlogia Prime."

I nodded. "Let me guess. The Zagrath have spread like a plague since we've been away?"

"The occupation has grown, Raas." Jorl stepped forward, touching a finger to the planet on the star chart. "We suspect at least two garrisons of soldiers."

"And the Carlogians?" I asked, not forgetting the most important factor. "Do we know if they welcome the Zagrath presence?"

Early in my career as Raas, I had forgotten that it did no good to rescue those who did not wish to be saved. I'd rashly led my warriors into battles where the natives had joined forces with the empire. After a few crushing defeats, I learned why the Vandar only interfered where there was a sizable resistance to imperial rule.

"They have issued distress calls." Symdar clenched his fists. "Not only are the Zagrath occupying their villages, they have conscripted the natives to work the mines they have built."

A low rumble issued from Jorl, and he flipped one of his braids over his shoulder. Although he was my *majak*, he was as eager for battle with the enemy as my battle chief.

"Then we will lend our blades to the people of Carlogia Prime," I said, then my gaze settled on Jorl. "I promised that the crew would get a chance to celebrate our victories, and I have not forgotten. After we crush this Zagrath encroachment, we will find ourselves a pleasure ship."

Symdar's eyes widened. "The crew will fight even more eagerly, if they know that females and wine are waiting for them."

"If we were close to Lissa, we could stop there," I said, with another glance at the star chart with its glowing blue and red dots. "But I'm afraid the crew's balls might fall off before we reach it."

Jorl laughed. "You might be right about that. We have been flying for a while without a break."

"A pleasure ship will be just as good as Lissa," Symdar assured me, though we both knew it was hard to match a pleasure planet for its variety.

Jorl smiled at me. "I will begin searching for such a ship, Raas." Then he cleared his throat and dropped his gaze to his feet. "Will you wish to reserve a pleasurer or two for yourself, Raas?"

"Why would I not?"

Symdar cocked an eyebrow at me. "You already have a female in your bed. I do not know how many you can take until it becomes too crowded."

I clapped a hand on my battle chief's shoulder. "That is something you should let me worry about."

"A good problem to have," Jorl added, although he did not look as convinced. He had experience with the female, and he knew she was not easily persuaded.

"Speaking of females," I said, leading them both to the door and walking onto the command deck with them. "I will be in my quarters. Let me know when we have reached Carlogia Prime."

They both clicked their heels together as I dismissed them and strode off toward my quarters again. I had not bathed since I'd returned from the raiding mission on the human's ship, and I wished to wash the grime from one battle off me before I went on another. I held no illusions that the female would join me in the bathing pools or wash me, but that did not mean I would avoid the pleasures that were my due as Raas.

Pressing my hand to the panel outside my quarters, I stepped inside, my gaze going to the bed. The empty bed.

It was only instinct that made me lift my arms to block the blow that came from one side. My hands grabbed the long handle, jerking the mangled battle axe toward me and bringing the female with it.

"*Tvek!*" I cursed, when she kicked at my shins, landing a blow and sending pain shooting up my leg.

I jerked the axe out of her hands completely and tossed it to the floor where it clattered loudly. Dodging behind me, she made a dash for the still-open door and was almost outside when I looped an arm around her waist and pulled her back in.

She flailed her arms, reaching for the sides of the round door as it slid shut. When she was locked inside with me again, I released her, and she dropped onto her hands and knees. Instead of giving up, the female dove for the axe on the floor and swung it up in a wild arc through the air.

The blade came so close to my leg that it sliced off one of the strips of leather that made up my battle kilt. Even she looked startled as the piece of dark leather hit the floor, her green eyes widening and her mouth falling open.

"You wish to kill me?" I asked, my voice a deadly purr as I advanced on her.

Even though I did not want to die at the hands of a human

female who'd clearly never swung an axe before, I did prefer her like this. I had wanted her fury instead of her practiced smiles, and I had gotten my wish.

"I want off." Her arms shook, as she tried to keep the axe high.

"What happened to our agreement? You agreed to come willingly if I spared your ship. I held up my end of the bargain."

She huffed out a breath. "I came willingly. I didn't agree to stay willingly."

I almost laughed. A clever trick of semantics. "My *majak* might argue that you did not even come on board willingly."

"Your *majak* can bite me."

I twitched one shoulder up. "Do not tempt him. At one point in our history, the Vandar used our teeth in battle. It would not be a stretch for him to bite you."

She narrowed her eyes at me and shook her head. "You're making that up."

I circled her, watching as her own steps became slower, and her arms drooped. The heavy weapon was too large for her. Even adult Vandar males trained for a long time to be able to wield a battle axe—and she was clearly not a male. Or Vandar. "I already told you, female. A Raas does not lie."

A rivulet of sweat trailed down her forehead. "My name is Tara. Not female."

"Fine, Tara." It was hard to watch her brandishing a battle axe in her nearly nonexistent clothing without getting aroused. Especially since her pale skin was flushed with exertion and her chest heaved, making her breasts quiver.

I had not drawn my own battle axe because I recognized the warped one she held as one of the weapons that had been crossed over my bed. How she'd ripped it off the wall was a mystery, but when I'd glanced at my bed, there was clearly a missing axe from the crossed weapons displayed above the headboard. I also knew that she would not have the strength to swing the heavy iron weapon again. Not with any kind of force that could do damage. Now, I was waiting for her to drop it from exhaustion.

"You say you want off my ship?" I continued to circle her, making her move to follow me. "I could always put you out an airlock. That would be the usual punishment for anyone who made an attempt on the Raas' life."

She bit her bottom lip. "I didn't try to kill you."

My gaze went to the bit of my kilt she'd sliced off.

"Slashing your skirt doesn't count."

"My skirt?" I glanced down at the battle kilt that had been worn by Vandar warriors for over a millennia. "This is a battle kilt, fe—Tara."

"Battle kilt, whatever. You got what you wanted, right? You punished a ship that ran supplies for the empire. You stripped my ship and took everything from me." She rested the circular blade of the axe on the floor, her shoulders slumping. "There's no reason for you to keep me here. Unless you plan to kill me, and if that's the case, I wish you'd just fucking do it."

I caught the handle of the axe as it slipped from her hand and caught her before she collapsed to the floor, my arm circling her waist and my tail wrapping around her legs as I pulled her flush to my body. "You are very wrong, Tara. There are many reasons for me to keep you here, and killing you is not one of them."

CHAPTER SEVEN

Tara

Even though my legs were like jelly, I stiffened when he pulled me close, his body cupping mine from behind. His thick arm held me around the waist, and his other hand stroked the side of my face.

My practical brain told me there was nowhere to run on the Vandar ship, but I couldn't just give in to him. Even if his touch scorched my skin and made my heart hammer in my chest.

"What made you think I would want to kill you?" he whispered, his lips buzzing against my ear.

"Because you're Vandar." I attempted to wiggle in his grasp but his grip on me tightened. "That's what you do, isn't it?"

His huge hand splayed across my bare stomach as he pulled me closer, and my feet almost left the floor. "I have killed many warriors before. And many Zagrath collaborators."

I gritted my teeth as he nestled his head in the crook of my neck and inhaled deeply. "I thought you considered me a collaborator worthy of death."

"Perhaps," he murmured, stroking my bare leg with the furry tip of his tail. "But I've never encountered a collaborator quite as soft as you, or one who smells good enough to eat."

I flinched. So, he thought I was soft? Irritation boiled inside me. I'd kept myself and my sister alive in an unforgiving and unkind galaxy—sacrificing and working myself to the bone—and he dared to call me soft?

When he lifted his head from my throat, I slammed my own head back hard, catching him off guard.

"*Tvek!*" he bellowed, dropping me and clutching his forehead.

The back of my head ached where I'd made contact with him, but I knew it didn't hurt as much as his. I staggered forward after being released so suddenly, but quickly regained my balance and spun around. Assuming a battle stance, I watched him straighten with one hand still on his head.

Instead of looking enraged, he was grinning. "If this is how you wish to play it, Tara."

"I'm not playing," I said.

He removed his hand from his head where a red knot was already blooming. "No?" Keeping his eyes locked on me, the Raas started to unhook the straps across his chest and drop them to the floor. As he removed each coil of black leather and metal, more of the dark markings on his chest were revealed.

"What are you doing?"

He slipped off first one scaled shoulder cap and then the other. "Preparing to win."

I gulped as I got my first full glimpse of his bare chest and arms. The alien was solid muscle—and lots of it. Even his stomach was a series of ripples disappearing beneath his kilt.

Please keep that on, I thought as I eyed the leather strips that reached halfway down his enormous thighs. I'd already felt what was beneath it, and I wasn't sure if I could handle seeing it right then.

"I can't have you attempting to kill me all the time," he said.

"I get that from the empire. I don't need it in my own quarters." I took a step away from him. "So, put me in the brig."

He tilted his head at me. "Vandar don't have a brig. We don't keep prisoners. If you commit an offense bad enough to be imprisoned, we put you out an airlock."

Shit. I really hadn't thought this through.

Before I could come up with another suggestion, he shook his head. "I brought you on board. I have to handle you, which means I need to teach you how a female should behave when she is with a Raas of the Vandar."

I choked out a laugh. "You're going to teach me how to act? You're kidding right? I'm the captain of my own ship."

"Not anymore you're not." He took a step toward me. "You're a guest on my ship. A guest who agreed to come willingly, I should add."

"Yeah, well." My gaze wandered to the expanse of bare flesh advancing on me. "I didn't agree to do everything willingly."

"No, you didn't." His top lip curled. "But you will."

"Dream on, Muscles." I scanned the room for any other ways out, but there was only the large arched door, which I knew was locked from the inside.

His brows lifted briefly before he lunged for me. I dodged to the side, barely skirting his reach. I didn't have long to celebrate because he was coming for me again, taking long strides with his jaw tight.

I ran to the bed and jumped on it, then ran across and hopped down on the other side. The Raas didn't bother crossing over the top of the bed. In a few steps he was rounding the foot of the bed.

Shit, shit, shit. This was definitely not going well. There was nowhere for me to run, and I seemed to be aggravating him more and more.

I took one look at his stormy expression and dashed for the bathroom, even though I knew there were even fewer places to hide in there. I'd peeked into the black-stone room briefly and marveled at the half-moon shaped tub filled with different colored water, but I hadn't even dipped my toes in.

Running around the tub, I faced off with him on the other side. When I saw the grin teasing his lips, I glared at him. "Are you enjoying this?"

"It is rare I find a worthy adversary."

My heart pounded as I gaped at him. "And that's what I am? An adversary?"

His pupils darkened. "What would you call us? We are not yet lovers."

"Don't hold your breath for that one," I muttered.

His brow furrowed for a moment, then he moved swiftly to close the gap between us, stepping over part of the tub.

Startled, I backed up and my foot slipped, sending me flying back and my arms pinwheeling to the sides. Before I hit the floor, the Raas caught my arms. I should have been grateful he didn't let me smack the hard stone, but I wasn't.

Instead of jerking me to him like I expected, the Raas lifted me into the air and lowered me quickly into the icy-blue water at the end of the segmented tub. The freezing water enveloped me up to my chin, the cold a shock to my system. My breath stalled in my chest and my entire body spasmed in response to the ice water—my legs going numb almost instantly.

Screaming, I thrashed in the water as he held my arms. "Let me out of here, you fucking sadist!"

As rapidly as he'd dunked me in the water, he pulled me out again, setting me on the dark stone.

Water puddled at my feet as it streamed off my body, and I

shivered violently. "I can't believe you did that." My teeth chattered, making my words hard to understand. "You bastard."

His hands still held my arms, and he lifted me, carrying me to the long, stone counter and setting me on it. "You needed cooling off."

My gaze went to the crescent-shaped tub with dividers separating the different colors of water. "Is that your idea of a relaxing bath? Are the Vandar really that messed up?"

His gaze didn't leave me. "It is not all cold. If you behave, I will show you the hot sections. They are quite pleasurable."

I shook my head as my teeth rattled. "No, thanks. I've had enough of Vandar bathing for now."

Without a word, he parted my legs and tugged me toward him so that I was straddling his waist. I tried to jerk back, but he wrapped his arms around me and flattened me to him. Even though I wanted to wrestle out of his grip, his body was so warm that I stopped fighting. Within moments, I'd stopped shivering, and my teeth no longer rattled in my head.

"Normally, I would say thank you, but you *are* the one who dunked me in the ice bath in the first place, so I should probably punch you in the gut."

"I would expect no less." He pulled away slightly, looking down at me. He moved one large hand up to cup my jaw, his gaze on my mouth.

My pulse fluttered wildly. I should have wanted to punch him, but I didn't. I wanted his lips on mine, and his body warming me again.

It's hypothermia, I thought. The effects of hypothermia were definitely making me delusional. There was no way I wanted this, my mind told me as he lowered his mouth to mine, and I sank into the kiss with a small moan. No fucking way in hell, I reminded myself as I wound my arms around his neck. I'm obviously still in shock, I said to myself as I opened my mouth to his and let his tongue caress mine with more tenderness than should have been possible from such a brute. Tangling my fingers in his hair, I assured myself that the pounding desire would soon pass—like a bad case of Virillian flu.

Then the ship pitched to one side, and sirens began to wail.

CHAPTER EIGHT

Kaalek

I grasped the metal handrail and hoisted myself up the staircase as the ship lurched again. As soon as I realized my ship was under attack, I'd left Tara and run for the command deck. She would be safe in my quarters, and I needed to get to the command deck and find out what had happened.

I'd hated having to pull away from her, especially when I'd seen the dazed look of desire in her eyes as she'd gazed up at me, her lips bruised by my kisses and her skin flushed. If she hadn't nearly slid down the entire length of the bathing chamber's counter, I might not have noticed the rough movement of the ship. I'd been so lost in the feel and taste of her.

Another blast sent me skidding down a suspended walkway, the metal hull of the ship groaning from the impact as my tail looped around a railing to catch me.

"*Tvek,*" I cursed under my breath. "It has to be the Zagrath."

No one else had the firepower to match us, although I couldn't imagine how they'd located us. Vandar warbirds were famous for our invisibility shielding. It was why we made such effective raiders. Our enemy couldn't see us coming. You couldn't defend yourself from an invisible foe that appeared out of the dark sky like a phantom.

I stormed onto the command deck, taking in the frenzied activity. Things did not appear to be going well.

"Raas." My *majak* made his way over to me, bracing himself on a standing console. His gaze flicked to my completely bare chest, but he did not mention my lack of shoulder armor—or the knot on my head. "I tried to contact you in your quarters, but the female said you'd already left."

"What is this?" I asked, raising my voice to a near-shout to be heard over the noises of battle. "Isn't our shielding working?"

My battle chief joined us, bracing his legs wide as the ship swayed. The fast swish of his tail revealed his agitation. "It's working, but an imperial fleet still found us."

An entire fleet. That explained the heavy fire.

"Impossible," I said, glaring at the view screen, as if my narrowed eyes could banish the gunmetal-gray battleships currently massed in front of us.

Symdar shook his head. "Not if they have another way to pinpoint our location."

"Another way?" My gaze did not leave the view screen, and I watched as ships from my horde flew wildly around the enemy battleships. At least our amoeba defense seemed to be keeping the Zagrath fleet occupied and confused.

Symdar lowered his voice, although it was still louder than usual. "The female."

I rubbed my head, the spot where she'd hit me tender. "The one in my quarters?"

Symdar exchanged a glance with Jorl. "She carried supplies

for the Zagrath. Who is to say she is not a spy for them, as well? She might have been sent to infiltrate our ship and send our coordinates to the fleet."

"How?" I eyed my battle chief. "You saw what she had on. There was no place to hide any sort of device. And did you not see her fight against coming with us? If her mission was to get onboard this ship, she did everything she could not to carry it out."

"That is what I thought, Raas," Jorl said, "but Symdar has a point. We have never been tracked by the enemy before. Now, as soon as the human is on our ship, they know where we are as if we are transmitting a homing signal."

I saw one of my horde ships taking heavy fire and strode to a nearby console. "Fly a defensive pattern around that vessel," I instructed the warrior standing next to me.

He clicked his heels together sharply. "Yes, Raas."

His fingers tapped expertly across the console and soon our warbird was dipping beneath the horde ship and coming between it and the Zagrath ship firing on it.

"Give them everything we've got," I told him.

He gave a single nod, firing a volley of laser fire across their bow. The enemy ship retreated.

"Our horde ship is safe," the warrior next to me said as I clapped him on the shoulder.

"It seems like they're only firing on some of our horde ships," I said, rejoining my *majak* and battle chief. "Do you see that?"

Symdar beckoned me to his standing console, pointing to a flashing readout of our horde, the hits they'd taken, and their weapon supply. "Aside from our lead ship, only three others appear to be the target of the Zagrath weapons."

"Because they can only detect three." I tapped my chin. "Why?"

Jorl leaned closer to the screen. "Those are the ships that also took some of the supplies we raided from the freighter."

My skin went cold. "You are sure?"

My *majak* gave a firm nod. "I directed the dispersion myself."

"So, it's not the female's presence on the ship that is a homing beacon," I said, squeezing my hands into fists. "It is her cargo. Zagrath cargo."

Both my *majak*'s and battle chief's faces were grim when I looked up. They were thinking what I could not say out loud. Even if the female was not a spy, her cargo had been a trap. Had she been the lure? A pretty girl barely dressed to distract us—to distract me—so we would let our guard down? Had this been her plan all along? Was Tara a part of the Zagrath plan, or was she just an unwitting accomplice?

"Raas," Jorl said. "We could not have known. You could not have—"

I cut him off with a slash of my hand. "Do not make apologies for me, *majak*. It was my decision to chase after the freighter."

"But we have raided countless ships and never been tracked before," Symdar said.

"Because they have never known where we would strike. It would be impractical to place trackers inside so many shipments moving through every sector." I swallowed down disgust at myself. "But this time they knew they had a target that the Vandar wanted."

A target that *I* had wanted, is what I did not say. A target I had insisted on chasing, even though it was not our fight. A target that had led us into a bloody battle. A battle we should not have been in. Not if I had not wanted to prove myself so much.

I growled low, thinking of what my father would say, what he would call me. Impulsive. Arrogant. Foolish.

Pushing aside the sound of my father's disapproval in my mind, I snapped my head up. "Tell the other ships to dump the cargo. Vent it into space and then blow it the *tvek* up. We can show them what we think of their trackers."

Symdar and Jorl both clicked their heels together, Jorl moving off toward the door.

I grabbed his arm. "Where are you going, *majak?*"

"Some of our systems have been damaged in the attack. I need to vent the cargo bay manually."

"I will do it," I told him.

He cocked his head at me, shaking it slightly. "But Raas—?"

I put up a hand to stop his protests. "It was I who got us into this. I should be the one to get us out."

He nodded, even though I could tell he was not happy with my decision. "What about the female? What if she was implanted with a tracker?"

I had not thought of that, and the idea fired my anger and made the tip of my tail quiver "There is only one way to know for sure. I will have to get her off the ship."

"You will vent her with the cargo?" Jorl hesitated as he asked this, and I could see in his eyes that he hoped this was not my plan.

"No, I will fly her off the ship in my fighter. If she is being tracked, I will know because the Zagrath will follow us or fire at us. If I can fly undetected with my invisibility shielding, then I will know she is not being tracked."

His brow furrowed. "Are you sure, Raas? This is a big risk. Should not I or one of the other warriors do this?"

I grasped his arm, holding it for a long moment. "It is not your task. I need you to be ready to take the horde to the rendezvous point. As soon as the cargo is destroyed, you should be able to fly without being followed. I will meet you there."

Even though he did not look pleased at any of this, he did not argue. "Yes, Raas. We will reunite at the rendezvous point."

I gave a quick look at the command deck and the warriors

intent of the battle before turning on my heel and walking quickly off. I broke into a jog as I made my way through the ship. There was no time to waste. I needed to get the enemy cargo off my ship.

But I needed to do something else first.

CHAPTER NINE

Tara

When he burst into the room, his eyes were wild. He stalked over to where I was sitting on the edge of the bed, my arms spread wide for balance as the ship rocked, and he pulled me up so that my chest bumped his.

"Did you know?" He shook me slightly as he spoke, and his dark eyes were pitch black with fury.

I tried to shake him off. "Know what? Have you gone insane?"

He jerked me so that our faces were so close I could have confused his ragged breath for my own. His gaze bored into me. "That the Zagrath cargo had trackers? Did you know?"

What? The Zagrath had tracked the cargo that had been in my freighter?

I shook my head. "No. I don't know what you're talking about. I swear it."

His eyes didn't leave mine, but he relaxed his grip. "If you're lying to me—"

"I'm not lying," I said. "I swear on the memory of my parents and the life of my sister."

He glared at me for a minute more before some of the anger left his gaze. He let me go and spun around. "Why would you lie? You haven't been shy about how you feel about the Vandar, or me. At least, not after you gave up that ridiculous attempt to seduce me."

I sank back down on the bed—trying not to be offended that he'd referred to my seduction attempt as ridiculous—while he opened an inset cabinet and dug around in a drawer.

He tossed a couple of handfuls of fabric back at me without turning around. "Put these on."

The clothes were clearly his and nothing short of enormous, but anything was better than wearing wet underwear. I considered peeling off my damp bra and panties before putting on the new clothes, but I didn't want to give the Raas anything more to look at. At least he was busy pulling on his own chest straps and shoulder armor and didn't seem to be paying attention to me.

Slipping on the huge black vest, I frowned when I saw that the two sides didn't close in the front. Just great. The skirt wasn't much better. It looked like the battle kilt he wore, but it was made out of a nubby fabric and the waist fell to my hips. If my ass hadn't been a little fatter than I would have liked, the thing wouldn't have stayed on me at all.

"*Vaes!*" He gave me a quick once-over as he took long steps toward the door, stopping halfway to pivot and motion for me to follow him. "Come!"

I didn't move as the ship shuddered. "Where are you taking me?"

He huffed out a breath and stomped over to me, grabbing me by the wrist and dragging me behind him. "You were so eager to get off my ship. Well, now you have your wish."

I stopped resisting and followed him out of the room. "You're letting me go?"

He cut his eyes to me, something flickering behind them for a moment. "In a way."

I wasn't crazy about how that sounded. Had he finally decided to put me out an air lock?

Before I could ask him to explain, the ship tilted, and we were slammed against a metal railing. My foot slipped and went over the side of the suspended walkway. Before the rest of me followed, and I fell through the web of walkways and staircases into the dark bowels of the ship, Kaalek jerked me back—one hand around my wrist and his tail coiled around one of my legs.

My heart raced as I peered over the side. I might have landed on a metal bridge below, or I might have missed it and plummeted hundreds of meters. "What kind of ship is this?" I cried. "Why is everything so open? You could kill yourself just trying to get from one place to the next!"

"It is a Vandar warbird," he said, as if that was explanation enough.

"Well, your warbird needs more fucking guardrails," I mumbled as I followed him, not minding the firm grip he had on my wrist. "Or walls."

I tried to keep up with the Raas' long strides, but it was hard not to be shaken by my near plummet over the edge. We ran down one walkway after another, passing Vandar warriors in full battle gear. The sirens had not ceased wailing, but I'd gotten used to the piercing noise.

"You still haven't told me where we're going," I yelled.

He swept me up in one arm and leapt down a flight of stairs, landing with the grace of a cat. He straightened and put me back on the floor. "The Zagrath followed the cargo and you. We are getting both off this ship. Once there is no way for the empire to track us, the odds will be even again."

My stomach hardened into a knot. "Are you saying the Zagrath Empire put a tracker in me?"

He looked at me for the first time since we'd started our journey through the ship. "I do not think so. I have never heard of them tracking living creatures, although I would not put it past them. To them, we are all disposable, unless we provide revenue to feed their greed."

I thought back to the last few times I'd had any encounters with the empire. Aside from picking up the cargo as instructed on Sellerian III, I hadn't laid eyes on an imperial soldier or envoy. The cargo had been waiting for me at an outpost, with only a guard checking the crates off a list as my crew had loaded them up. The guard had seemed pretty uninterested in anything but getting back to his game of parisa cubes. I couldn't imagine him being involved in any imperial plan.

But, clearly I'd been naïve about the empire. If they'd tracked the cargo they'd given me, that meant one of two things. Either they didn't trust me to deliver it, or they wanted it to get taken by Vandar raiders so they could use it to track them down.

Since I'd picked up the cargo after Astrid had been taken and had made no secret that I was still searching for my sister, I was pretty sure it was the latter. The Zagrath Empire had used my ship and my cargo as bait, and now I was in danger of being blown up because I'd led the empire right to us.

"Fucking bastards," I said under my breath as a double door slid open, and I found myself in a cargo bay filled with familiar steel barrels and stacks of crates. They all had the Zagrath seal on the side, and apparently trackers somewhere inside.

The Raas dropped my hand and hurried to a standing console, his fingers flying across the surface. Within seconds, he ran back to me and pulled me out of the room. The doors glided shut, and he punched a code into the side panel causing them to lock.

I peered through the clear panel in the doors as the far hatch of the cargo bay was vented into space and all the contents sucked out. I swallowed hard. I knew what was in the various containers—rations, fuel, fabric. All things that were needed desperately throughout the galaxy and controlled by the empire. But I knew the Raas had had no choice.

"It is done," he said, but his voice was not so harsh. "*Vaes.*"

Tearing my gaze from the crates floating in space, I let him lead me down another long walkway, through high, wide doors, and into a massive hangar bay.

Like the rest of the ship, it was all dark metal and exposed iron beams with a soaring ceiling, large enough to hold a small fleet of ships. I remembered arriving here before I was escorted to the Raas' quarters and spotted the transport that had brought us—or at least one that looked like it. There was a row of black, bird-like ships similar to the transport—all of them powering up as warriors rushed on board.

"You're sending out raiding parties?" I asked.

He gave a curt shake of his head. "Not raiding. Killing."

Ship after ship filled with Vandar warriors standing body to body, with arms clutching steel bars overhead and tails swishing menacingly by their feet. Ramps lifted and slammed shut. Engines fired and ships rocketed out of the hangar bay with a roar.

Nerves fluttered in my chest as the Raas pulled me onto a small ship, its ebony wings sleek and pointed. I still wasn't sure what he planned to do with me. "I thought you said I wasn't tracked."

The Raas strapped me in to one of the fighter's two front seats, taking the one next to me and flipping switches to engage the engine. "I said I *thought* you weren't tracked. If you are, I'll know soon enough."

I twisted around as the ramp to the ship slammed shut, the engine a throaty rumble beneath my feet "You're using me to draw fire?"

"I'm using *us*," he corrected. "If you don't have a Zagrath tracker, we'll be able to fly out using Vandar invisibility shielding, and none of the Zagrath ships will follow us. Then we'll rendezvous with my horde at the meet point."

"And if I do have a tracker?" I asked as he gunned the engine, and we flew across the floor of the hangar bay, the force pushing me into my seat.

The Raas glanced at me, his expression intense and his eyes sparking. "Then things might get rough."

CHAPTER TEN

Kaalek

"Rough?" Her hands gripped the armrests as we burst out of the warbird.

I banked hard right, flying around the side of my ship and dodging the cargo floating in space. The blackness was illuminated by the red glow of laser fire, and the occasional explosion that flamed gold before being doused. Vandar ships darted around the Zagrath battleships, a few latching onto the hulls.

I could imagine the familiar sound of scraping metal as they cut through the hull to board the enemy ship, and I wished I was with them. There was nothing like the adrenaline rush of pouring onto an imperial ship, blades flashing.

Checking to be sure my invisibility shielding was activated, I flew the fighter away from the action. If Tara had any sort of tracker embedded in her, they would be able to hone in on me, even if I was invisible to sensors.

I didn't like being away from the action, and it seemed

cowardly to be hovering beyond the fighting. I flew a larger arc around the battle, as if I was circling an opponent. I'd never viewed a Vandar-Zagrath battle this way, and it was strange to witness the chunky, gray imperial battleships firing at nothing and lasers and torpedoes being returned from what looked like empty space. Our invisibility shielding did make us unseeable until we fired, yet the Zagrath had found us using the tracked cargo. I almost admired their strategy, even as rage bubbled inside me.

Hovering on the outskirts of battle, I waited. No ships flew out to intercept us, and no laser fire was directed our way. I exhaled, more relieved than I wanted to admit. It appeared that the female was not a living tracker. It had not been her who had led the Zagrath to us. Her cargo, yes, but not her body.

Chancing a furtive glance at her, I wondered what I would have done if she had been tracked. I know what would have been expected of me, but I wasn't sure if I could have done it. I let out another long breath, glad my ruthlessness had not been put to the test.

It wasn't that I cared for her, I told myself. But I did find her and her inability to back down from a fight to be intriguing. She was a valiant—if inexperienced—fighter, and I relished the thought of conquering a female who fought me so ruthlessly. I never would have suspected that I liked a female who challenged me, but rebuffing her attempts to attack me had been the most fun I'd had in a long time. The fact that she made my cock hard every time I touched her was an added bonus.

"So?" Tara said, her voice unsure. "Can they see us or not?"

She tugged the two halves of her leather vest together, but the black of her bra still flashed in the space where they didn't meet. I concentrated on the ship's controls and tried not to remember the softness of her skin and how her breasts had quivered in my hands. I needed to focus on my mission, not on the female next to me and how much I wanted to bury my cock inside her.

I brought the nose of the ship around so that we could assess the battle. "It seems they cannot."

She blew out a breath and unclenched the armrests. "Do you believe me now? I told you I wasn't a spy for the empire."

"I believe that you do not have a tracker implanted in you." I did not believe she was a spy, but I did not want to let her off so easy. Not when she had been working for the enemy. "Whether you have been spying for the Zagrath is another question."

She rolled her head back against the seat. "Seriously? What do I have to do to prove to you that I'm not spying for the empire? I hate the bastards as much as you do."

I held up a hand to stop her. "Unless your planet has been stripped bare and your people enslaved to their greed, you do not hate them as much as I do."

Silence hung between us until she finally cleared her throat. "Does the empire still control Vandar?"

I shook my head, not meeting her gaze. "We abandoned our home world generations ago, but only after the Zagrath had mined it for any natural resource that could be monetized, and made my people work like dogs just to survive on their own planet. They did not count on us being clever, though. They also did not count on us being able to build ships to take us off the planet. It cost many Vandar their lives, but our hordes escaped and took to the skies." I waved a hand at the battle before us. "We have been fighting the empire ever since so that they do not gain control of the galaxy."

"So, every Vandar lives in one of your flying hordes? What about the women?"

I cut my eyes to her. "We have secret colonies—far from these sectors—where our people live in peace away from Zagrath rule. That is where raiders go once we retire our battle axe."

"I've never heard of secret Vandar colonies."

"They would not be much of a secret if every human in league with the empire knew about them."

She bristled at my description of her, but didn't argue. Peering out the front of the ship, she jumped when the Vandar shuttles and transports peeled off the imperial battleships and returned to the warbirds, seeming to vanish as they entered the invisible ships. Then the laser fire erupting from the cloaked Vandar ships ceased. The horde had left the battle for the rendezvous point.

Tara tilted her head at me. "I don't suppose you want to tell me how you guys do that?"

I almost laughed at her boldness, as I engaged the thrusters and moved us into the path I knew my horde had taken. "No, I do not, *spy*."

She huffed out a breath. "How many times do I have to tell you—?" She did not get to finish her protest as the fighter we were in listed sharply to one side. She braced her arms against the console as we were both jerked out of our seats, the chest straps the only things keeping us from flying free. "What the fuck was that?"

The pilot's console flashed with red warnings, but I didn't need to look at them to know what had happened. I could smell the familiar scent of scorched steel. "We were hit."

"I thought you said the Zagrath couldn't see us."

I shot her a look before turning my attention to the controls. "I did not think they could. We might have taken stray laser fire." One problem with being positioned near a battle was the possibility of weapons going astray. "Nothing else is incoming, so we should be fine. We only sustained minor damage. If we fly on impulse—"

Tara reached over and slapped at my arm. "I don't think that's good."

I glanced up, following her gaze. My skin went cold. A hulking, gray chunk of a destroyed Zagrath ship was spiraling toward us.

Tvek. I sent more power to our rear thrusters, firing them in hopes of getting us out of the way in time to avoid the flying debris. Our fighter lurched forward, and I jammed the controls to bank it to one side, but the fire we'd taken had made the engines sluggish. We were not going to be able to outrun the impact. "Brace!"

Tara threw her arms out as the hull of the imperial ship caught our wing, knocking us backward and sending us cartwheeling.

The safety straps strained across my shoulders and chest, cutting into my bare flesh as I was tossed up and down from the spin. Tara's scream was piercing, but at least it let me know she was okay.

When the fighter stopped flipping, I gave my head a quick shake, peering out the front of the ship. We'd been knocked far away from the battle. The Zagrath ships looked tiny, and there was no sign of my horde. No doubt they'd flown at warp once they'd departed, so they'd missed seeing my ship get shot then hit by flying enemy debris.

No matter. I glanced at Tara, who had a hand to her head. "Are you hurt?"

"I don't think so, but I might throw up."

"Please do not." I peered at my console. There were even more flashing alert lights. *Tvekking* hell. It looked like we'd lost thrusters entirely, and we had a fuel leak.

"No problem," she said, her tone acerbic. "I'll just hold it."

I ignored her mumbled complaints as I assessed the damage to the fighter and our best options. Navigational controls appeared to be functional, as well as long-range scanners. Unfortunately, they showed me nothing but a bunch of imperial ships. Not an option. I would rather die in space than request assistance from the enemy.

A faint dot blinked blue on the star chart. It was at the edge of our possible range, but if I flew steadily and our fuel held out, we should be able to make it. I set in a course, touching a finger to the dot representing our destination.

"What's that?" Tara asked, her gaze locking on my finger.

"We're going to make a pit stop on Carlogia Prime."

CHAPTER ELEVEN

Tara

"I don't understand," I cried, as the fighter hurtled toward the surface of the planet. "I thought we had enough fuel to get to Carlogia Prime."

The ship rattled as we plunged through the cerulean-blue haze that swirled above the planet. Raas Kaalek swiped his fingers across the console in front of him, but the alarms continued to screech.

"We had just enough fuel to get us to the planet," he said over the noise. "I never said we had enough to help steady our descent."

"Are you fucking kidding me?" My knuckles were bone-white as I clutched the armrests. "Crash landing on a planet is not the same as arriving safely."

"I am aware of that, female." His jaw was tight, and he didn't glance at me.

We were back to the "female" thing again. Since we were

about to crash in a flaming ball of hellfire, I decided not to quibble with him. I sucked in a breath. "Do I smell something burning?"

"Our hull might be igniting on the approach."

"Might be?" I swiveled my head around, expecting to see a wall of flames out the side of the fighter. There wasn't one, but that didn't mean something wasn't burning since the smell of smoke was getting stronger. "Isn't a burning hull something you should know for sure?"

Kaalek grunted in response.

The flashing console told me that the systems were severely damaged. Most of them were blinking a series of random symbols and other readouts were garbled lines of code streaming across the screen.

After passing through the thick, blue haze, we dropped into the planet's lower atmosphere. I'd never heard of Carlogia Prime before—primarily because it was located in a sector I didn't frequent—but I was surprised by how habitable the planet looked. Although we were passing by the terrain extremely rapidly, I saw lush forests and huge lakes of sea-green water. I didn't spot any cities, or even any signs of towns, but I wasn't sure which part of the planet was populated.

All I knew was what the Raas had told me during our voyage to the planet. Carlogia Prime was an independent planet that had not attained warp technology or even much of any technology, but they'd recently been colonized by the empire. It was a planet with a sizable population of Carlogians and an even greater supply of rare core minerals. According to Kaalek, the empire was after both the rare minerals they needed to power their technology and the alien population to mine it for them.

I'd asked him if the natives were barbarians since they were not technologically advanced, but he'd only shaken his head, his brow furrowed. Not comforting.

I put my fingers to my lips as the ship dropped sharply. If I'd thought I was going to be sick after our ship had somersaulted, I really felt like losing my lunch now. I forced myself to keep my eyes open as our ship brushed over the tops of trees, dropping faster every second.

"I hope this works," the Raas muttered as he tapped away at the screen.

I didn't have time to ask him what he meant, before the fighter jerked back as if it had been tugged by a string. The thrust seemed to have slowed our forward momentum, and we almost hovered in air before starting to glide forward again, this time more slowly.

"I don't know what you did, but it was—" I didn't get the chance to tell him that I'd been impressed by his trick before we crashed through a copse of trees. Branches scraped the hull, but the ship didn't stop, plowing through the lush forest and skimming across a pond. Water flew up behind us as the bottom of the hull bounced a few times, rattling my teeth and slamming me up and down, before hitting the pink-sand beach on the other side, flipping over once and skidding to a stop.

Kaalek and I hung upside down from our safety restraints. The sirens spluttered out, and then there was only the sound of our heavy breathing.

"That was not the worst landing I have had," he said, after a moment.

I stared at him from my inverted position, my hair hanging so that it almost touched the ceiling. "Then remind me not to go on any more ships with you."

"If it wasn't for you, I would not have had to take out the fighter."

"This is my fault?" I tried to glare at him as all the blood continued to rush to my head. "If you'd believed me, neither of us would be in this position."

"How was I supposed to believe you, when your cargo was

what led the empire to my horde?" His voice was a bellow that filled the cockpit.

"I told you I didn't have anything to do with that. I'm just as much of a victim of the empire in all this as you are."

He shook a finger at me then started to work the clasps on his safety straps. "No, you collaborated with the empire. And now you don't like it when you discover that they've deceived and used you. But it was always your choice to work for them."

"It's not that simple." Now I was screaming as loud as he was. "I did what I had to do to survive and keep my sister alive. Maybe you aren't crazy about your family, but that's your deal. I had to take care of mine, so I made sacrifices and did things I hated. And frankly, I don't give a teeny, tiny rat's ass if you approve of my decisions, but I didn't have anything to do with that cargo, and I didn't lie to you."

I heaved in a breath. Shit. I'd just screamed at a huge, Vandar warlord who wore a battle axe and had a fierce temper. I forced myself not to look away from him.

He'd stopped yanking on his straps and stared baldly at me. "Teeny tiny rat's ass?"

Even with the blood rushing to my face, heat creeped up my neck. "I think you got my point."

"I did." He pulled again on his straps and they came loose. He spun gracefully in mid-air and landed in a crouch on the ceiling. Turning to me, he nodded to my straps. "I can help you."

"I've got it." I tugged at my own, expecting them to be stuck. They weren't. I dropped instantly, not flipping gracefully, and instead landing in a heap on the hard ceiling, a sharp pain shooting up from my ankle.

Kaalek bent to help me up. "Your hostility is only matched by your stubbornness."

I waved him off as he tried to hoist me up. "I think I twisted my ankle when I landed." Reaching down, I touched my ankle and flinched from the pain. "Yep. It's twisted, all right."

The Vandar warlord frowned at me. "Are all human females as difficult as you are? I cannot imagine my brother dealing with this."

I snapped my head up to meet his gaze. "You mean the brother who took my sister?" My throat tightened at the thought of Astrid, and how scared she must be. Astrid was not tough, and she was not difficult, and I hated to think what she'd been forced to do because she wouldn't have had the courage to stand up for herself. "I hope she's giving him hell."

He snorted a laugh. "That is not what she is giving him."

Fresh anger flared inside me. How dare he joke about my sister and his brute of a brother? "What the fuck does that mean?"

He met my eyes, amusement evident in his. "I mean that your sister and my brother now share mating marks."

"I don't know what that means." But I didn't like the sound of it. "Mating marks? Did he brand her?"

He sighed, as if my questions were tedious. "All Vandar males are born with marks." He pointed to the swirling black lines that curved around his own chest muscles. "When we find our true mate, the marks appear on her skin and our marks extend until the markings on our bodies are perfectly matched."

I gaped at him, not bothering to close my mouth. "You're kidding, right? Are you trying to tell me that my sister and a Vandar warlord share mating marks? That they're fated to be together?"

He shrugged, as if he were not nearly as nonplussed as I was. "I have seen them myself or I would not have believed a human female could have bonded with a Vandar, especially a Raas."

"Does that mean my sister...?" I let my words fade out even as I tried to imagine tentative Astrid with the massive Vandar raider I'd seen take her off the ship.

"Fucked him?" His voice was low and silky, and snapped me out of my daze. "Of course."

"I don't believe it. Astrid would never... She was a... It's impossible."

He tilted his head at me. "I think you don't know your sister as well as you think you do. And I promise you I am telling the truth. Like I told you before, female. I do not lie."

"Tara." I scowled at him, angry at what he'd just told me and angry at the suggestion that I didn't know my own sister. What upset me most was that he might be right. The Astrid I knew could never have survived captivity with the Vandar, much less formed mating marks with a Raas. I swung my gaze up at him, narrowing my eyes. "I hope you don't think that just because my sister bonded with your brother that anything is going to happen between us."

He scooped me up off the ground, ignoring my swats to his chest. "At this point, I am just trying to survive you."

CHAPTER TWELVE

Kaalek

"Must you hit me, female… I mean, Tara?" I carried her out of the upside-down ship, stepping over the ledge created when the ship's hatch opened but extended high into the air instead of toward the ground.

"Well, yeah. You can't carry me around like I'm some helpless woman." She slapped at my chest again, and I suppressed the urge to drop her on her ass. "You didn't even ask if you could pick me up."

If I didn't already wish I'd never pursued the human's freighter, this would have settled it. As physically appealing as she was, she was more trouble than I ever could have expected —even when she wasn't lunging for me with an axe.

"You'd rather I left you on the ship?" I didn't roll my eyes at her, but it took restraint. "You cannot walk."

Before she could argue further, she drew in a breath and clamped a hand over her nose. "What is that smell?"

I'd been able to get basic environmental readings from the planet on our approach. The air was breathable, if a little thin, but the heavy blue haze that hung over the planet trapped in moisture and heat, making the air sticky. I assumed the humidity and greenery of our surroundings, coupled with the vibrant-green water in the nearby lake, gave the air its swampy scent.

"Welcome to Carlogia Prime." I walked to the edge of the sand, where trees popped out of the ground and the sand ceded to patches of greenery, and I plopped her down on a fallen log covered with purple shimmery moss. Then I straightened and adjusted my battle axe on my waist.

She swung her head around. "It looks pretty primitive."

"How many places have you been that haven't been outposts or colonies?"

She opened her mouth, then clamped it shut. "Actually, none. I've heard of beaches, but I've never actually been on one."

As she took in the strip of pink sand that faded into forest, I stood back, appraising the fighter.

Tvekking hell. It was a miracle we'd made it to the surface. The hull was scorched, and one of the wings clipped half off. Gashes scored the side of the ebony ship, and smoke poured from the exhaust vent.

I scraped a hand through my hair and tried to calm the twitching of my tail. We might have arrived in the Vandar fighter, but we weren't leaving in it. Even if I could somehow flip the ship over, it was in no way flyable.

Out of instinct, I leaned back and looked up at the sky, deep blue and diffusing the light of a single sun through its atmosphere. I could not see to space beyond, but I already missed the dark expanse—and my horde. By now, my raiders were far from here. Even though Carlogia Prime had been our original destination, my warriors would be waiting for me at the rendezvous point. A meeting I would not make.

It would not take Symdar and Jorl long to realize that something had happened to keep me. Per Vandar protocol, they had instructions to wait for a set amount of time before proceeding with a search. That meant I had at several standardized solar cycles before they would track us down. I twisted my neck from side to side. That was not too long, especially on a planet that seemed to be habitable. As long as I managed to avoid being spotted by the Zagrath who now occupied the planet. A Raas of the Vandar would not be a welcome visitor to anyplace controlled by the empire.

As angry as I was to be stuck on the planet, there was no use fuming about it. The faster I could get a distress call off the planet, the faster we could get rescued. *We.* I looked over at Tara as she sat on the fallen log, her injured leg stretched out in front of her. The small ankle was, indeed, swollen, and looked bluer than it had when I'd carried her outside.

I sighed. Her red curls fell into her face as she inspected her ankle, and she blew a tendril out of her eyes. She would not be able to travel on her hurt leg unless she allowed me to carry her, and that was questionable. I had no desire to walk while being struck repeatedly. But I also could not leave her, as much as I would have liked to.

"Does it hurt?" I asked.

She peered up at me, putting one hand over her eyes to shade them from the glare. "Not much."

I frowned. "Even though I have promised not to lie to you, you continue to tell me untruths. I can see the pain in your eyes."

She bit down on her lower lip. "Fine. It hurts. But I've had worse."

"You cannot walk on it," I said, not asking her.

"I could hop. But not very fast."

Again, I fought the desire to shake my head at the stubborn female. "We need to get away from the ship."

Her eyes widened, darting to the smoldering wreck of my ship. "Why? Is it going to blow?"

"No, but if the planet is being monitored—which it is, if it has Zagrath garrisons—then someone would have seen our arrival."

She pushed herself up, so she was partially standing. "And they would know that the ship streaking through the sky was a Vandar fighter."

I nodded, pleased that she'd picked up so quickly. Then again, she was a captain of a ship herself, and clearly had a mind for strategy.

"But why didn't they shoot us down?" she asked. "If the Zagrath are already here?"

"This is a new colony for them. If my guess is right, they have not had time to build air defenses. We were hoping to purge the planet of the Zagrath before they got their claws in too deeply. Once the empire sets up a defensive shield around a planet, our job is harder."

"So, they might not have seen us?"

"I am sure they saw us. My invisibility shielding was damaged, so we would have been completely visible. At the very least, we terrified the village we flew over before hitting the water." I took a step toward her, then stopped. "Since you cannot do much more than hobble, I need to carry you, if we are to put any distance between ourselves and the smoking ship."

She narrowed her eyes at me as if her injury had been part of some master plan of mine.

I folded my arms across my chest. "I could easily leave you here. You can meet the natives on your own and see how they welcome a female in a Vandar ship."

"You wouldn't," she said.

I cocked an eyebrow at her.

"Okay, you can carry me," she said, as if she were bestowing a great honor on me.

I lifted her easily, being careful not to jostle her injured leg. She readjusted her vest, which seemed to constantly flap open, and I kept my eyes up so as not to be tempted by a glimpse of her creamy skin.

All I wanted was to get us both off the planet and away from reach of the empire so I could return her to her sad freighter and never set eyes on her again. I didn't care if it meant returning to my brother's sector or tracking down the ship again. I was going to undo the mistake I'd made and send Tara on her way. If I was really feeling vindictive, I'd sneak her onto my brother's ship. Let the great Raas Kratos deal with this hellcat.

"What so funny?" she asked, as I tramped through the thick undergrowth.

I hadn't known I'd been laughing but I guessed the idea of my older brother juggling two human females had amused me. I only had one, and so far she'd tried to kill me and was the reason the empire had been able to track my horde and launch an attack. I couldn't imagine what she could do with more time or an accomplice.

"Nothing," I answered gruffly, glancing down and then away again when I saw that her kilt had ridden up so that most of her thighs were exposed. I remembered all too well the sheer sliver of black fabric covering her sex, and just the thought of it made my cock swell.

Tvek. Not only was I walking through an alien forest while carrying a female, I now had to do it with an aching cock. I shifted my grip on her, keeping my gaze focused on the trees ahead. Too bad my body hadn't gotten the message that Tara was nothing but trouble.

CHAPTER THIRTEEN

Tara

If there was any way I could have walked, I would have. Being carried by the bossy Vandar as he tramped through the thick forest was not my idea of a good time, even though he was careful about not bumping my ankle or jostling me too much.

I'd never been in an actual forest, and I was startled by how many strange sounds there were. After years spent on a spaceship, the chirps and caws were unusual to my ears. The swampy air made sweat trickle down my face, though I'd gotten used to the pungent scent, and my clothes had wilted in the humidity, the kilt no longer holding sharp creases.

I helped the Raas push the wide, fan-shaped leaves aside before we passed through them, but filmy tendrils of diaphanous greenery draped down from overhead and brushed my head. I swatted at both them and the occasional flying creature that buzzed near my ears.

"How do you do it?" I finally asked, my throat thick from thirst.

"Do what?" He glanced down at me then quickly up again before a green-blue frond smacked him in the face.

"Walk around in leather? Aren't you burning up?"

He gave me a curious look. "It is warmer than on my warbird, but I am not burning, as you suggest."

Black spots danced in front of my eyes, and I let my head rest on the firm plane of his chest. "You really are a superhuman wraith."

"Wraith?"

I cursed myself for letting that slip, although I was too tired and thirsty to care as much as I should have. "Just what people whisper about the Vandar raiders. That you're like ghosts appearing out of the blackness, bringing terror with you, and vanishing just as quickly. Only something unnatural could walk through this and not be gasping."

"We are not wraiths. We are fighting for freedom."

I twitched one shoulder as I let my eyes close. "To those you attack, you're a nightmare."

He was quiet for a few beats, the only sounds the crunching of leaves beneath his feet and the distant hoot of some creature. "If we are enough of a nightmare to the Zagrath, maybe they will cease their illegal actions."

I stifled a laugh. "Because life is fair like that."

Before he could respond, the Raas stopped and crouched, still holding me.

I opened my eyes, surprised that we had finally made it to the edge of the forest. Cleared land and some sort of village lay ahead. I didn't know much about the Carlogians, but it was clear from their village that they were far from barbarians. The central road through the village was hard-packed dirt, but it was lined with neat, two-level buildings that sat shoulder to shoulder—some made from stone and some from wood—with neatly shingled roofs and shuttered windows. In the center of the road was a square of some sort that boasted an obelisk not much higher than the buildings.

"Why are we stopping?"

Kaalek shushed me, which I did not like.

"Don't you—" I started to say, but he clamped a hand over my mouth.

Was this asshole seriously not letting me speak? Before I could peel his hand from my face, I saw why he'd wanted me to be quiet. Zagrath soldiers.

A pair in slate-blue uniforms with shiny, black helmets over their heads strode across the village's central street, disappearing into a stone building. I knew as well as he did that there would never be just two imperial soldiers. There were undoubtably more, even if we couldn't see them yet.

His hand relaxed over my mouth after I hadn't made a noise for a while, and then he dropped it. His face was tense as he scanned the village.

"What do we do?" I whispered. "Go back to the ship?"

He gave a brusque shake of his head. "No. If Zagrath soldiers are stationed this close to where we crashed, they've already found the ship."

My stomach clenched. "Which means they know a Vandar raider is somewhere on the planet."

He grunted in response, a muscle ticking in his jaw. "Especially since I activated a Vandar homing beacon. It's the only way my horde will be able to pinpoint us."

"But it also tells your enemy right where you are."

"That is the drawback." He shifted his feet as he crouched, still holding me in his arms. "We will just have to avoid the Zagrath until my horde arrives."

I gave him a pointed look. "How do you expect to do that? You don't exactly blend."

He scowled at me. "I didn't know we'd be crashing onto an alien planet, so I forgot to bring a costume change."

Since he'd been carrying me through the forest and was probably more tired and thirsty than I was, I let his smartass comment slide. "Well, we need food and water. Especially water."

He peered back into the dense greenery. "I could search for a water source. There must be a stream somewhere."

I shook my head. "That could take forever, and you don't know you'd be able to find one." I cut my eyes to the village. "We need to go there."

"I do not have any problem taking on the Zagrath soldiers, but once I kill them all, the empire will know exactly where we are. And they will send reinforcements."

I narrowed my eyes at him. "Who said anything about killing all the soldiers? Is that your only strategy? I meant that we could sneak in and find a place to hide."

"Hiding is no good. We need a healer for your leg." He glanced at my leg, then away again. "And you need to eat."

"My leg is fine," I argued. "It's more important that we don't get caught. At this point I'm conspiring with a Vandar raider, so I doubt I'd get a hero's welcome either."

"Me, they would execute."

I bobbled my head back and forth. "Probably."

He choked out a laugh. "Thank you for not lying to me about that."

I couldn't help the grin that escaped my lips. "I told you I would tell you the truth. I'm not a Zagrath spy, I had nothing to do with that cargo, but they would definitely kill you if they caught you."

The two imperial soldiers appeared from the building and strode down the main road away from us, their arms swinging by their sides. We watched in silence until they'd disappeared again.

"Maybe there are only two," I suggested.

Kaalek grunted again. "The Zagrath would never have only two fighters to control a village. There is a full garrison here. We just can't see them, yet."

I decided to take his word for it. Since he'd spent his life chasing after the Zagrath, I figured he knew them a bit better than I did.

"Where are all the residents of the village? The Carlogians, right?" I waved a hand at the village with its carefully crafted buildings and central tower. "Shouldn't there be some movement in the middle of the day?" I slapped a hand over my mouth. "You don't think the empire killed them all, do you?"

"No." Raas Kaalek's eyes were ominous. "They need them to work. The Zagrath always use the residents for the labor they need to strip planets dry. It's part of their cruelty to force the people to destroy their own home."

If everything he said about the empire was true—or even half of it—I understood why he hated them so much and felt sick that I'd ever worked for them. "Okay, so maybe they're all at work. That's good. It gives us time to sneak in without being seen."

The Raas stood and made a move to start walking, but I smacked his chest to stop him.

"Not like this," I told him when he scowled down at me. "I have a plan."

I ignored his eyebrow raised in obvious surprise. "I *was* a captain, remember?"

"I remember. I also remember that you won your title in a game of chance."

"Which is why you should listen to me. I know how to bluff and scheme." I gestured to his broad chest. "I don't have brawn, so I've always had to use my brains."

He studied me for a moment, then he let out a breath. "What is your plan?"

"Get me to the village, and then let me down. I'll go in myself as a wounded female. I should be able to find someone who'll be sympathetic. Then I'll come get you."

His scowl deepened. "I cannot send you in alone. What if you're taken by Zagrath soldiers?"

I put a hand on his chest. "Trust me. I can sweet-talk my way out of just about anything. Besides, I'm not planning to talk to any soldiers."

"That does not make me feel any better, female."

I glared at him.

"Tara," he corrected.

"You have a better plan?" I asked, then held up a finger before he could speak. "One that doesn't involve a bunch of dead bodies?"

The Raas pressed his lips together. "You say that as if it is a bad thing."

"Let's try it my way first. If it goes south, you can run in with your battle axe swinging."

That seemed to appease him. He grunted his assent, then without a word, he ran swiftly across the expanse of open land toward the village, flattening himself against the first building we reached. He lowered me to the ground, and my ankle twinged from the pressure as I tried to balance on two feet.

He furrowed his brow as he watched me. "You are sure about this?"

I wasn't, but no way was I going to let him know that. Like I'd said, I was a good bluffer. "Trust me."

Another unhappy grunt, but he did not move as I hobbled away from him and rounded the corner. The village road was still empty, and all the doors to the buildings closed. I kept one hand on a building wall as I hobbled, so I wasn't completely out in the open. Still, I thought I saw curtains flutter in high windows.

When I reached the first door, I tapped lightly on it. Nothing. I tapped again then tried the knob. Locked.

Peering around, I wondered if the entire village would be this way. I dreaded having to limp to every building. I sighed and turned to make my way to the next building, when the door suddenly opened behind me, and I was jerked inside, a blade held to my neck.

CHAPTER FOURTEEN

Tara

I barely breathed as strong arms held me and the blade pricked the skin on my neck. My eyes adjusted to the lower light inside the building, and I saw that it was a shop of some kind. Shelves lined one wall, and a large worktable was covered in scraps of fabric. A burning candle gave off the scent of tallow and made shadows dance on the walls.

"Who are you?" He spoke the universal tongue, but with a lilting accent I'd never heard before.

I couldn't see him, but the tenor of his voice told me he was older. "My name is Tara. I crash-landed on your planet and need some help."

His arms relaxed their grip, and the point of the blade left my neck. "Are you armed?"

"No. You can check me if you want."

He released me and backed up quickly. I turned with my

hands up. I'd never met a Carlogian, so I shouldn't have had any expectations, but I was still surprised by his appearance.

Short and stocky, with heavily lined skin the color of copper, the creature had horns that curved back from his forehead and wrapped around his ears. The horns themselves were beautiful, with stripes of rich pigment ringing them from the base to the pointy tips. I didn't dwell on his horns for too long, though, my gaze going naturally to his attire, which was impressive.

He was dressed more elaborately than anyone I'd ever seen, although my exposure *had* been limited to seedy outposts and Zagrath colonies, where uniforms were the norm. My crew had worn utilitarian pants and T-shirts, and the Vandar dressed like galactic Vikings. This alien put all of that to shame with his three-piece suit made out of a brown, nubby fabric. The pants were tapered into chestnut-leather, laced boots, the jacket was almost molded to him, and the waistcoat buttons looked like a row of intricate gold coins. A shimmery burgundy scarf ruffled up around his neck.

The Carlogian male eyed me up and down. "What are you?"

"Human." I realized I looked as strange to him as he did to me.

His large, brown eyes assessed me shrewdly as he tucked the stick pin he'd been holding at my neck into his scarf, revealing that it had a jeweled head. "Like the Zagrath?"

"I'm not Zagrath," I said, hoping this was the right thing to say. "We both descended from the same planet a long time ago, but I'm not one of them."

He seemed to accept this, walking behind his table and picking up a swath of cloth. "You arrived on the ship we saw fly through the air and leave a trail of smoke?"

"I guess so." I wasn't sure when I should mention that it was a Vandar ship, and I was accompanied by a raider warlord. "Did a lot of people in your village see it?"

His gaze flicked to the window that was covered by wooden shutters. "Everyone."

"Even the Zagrath soldiers?"

He met my eyes and gave me a single nod before turning his attention back to the cloth and smoothing it across the table. "Many of them went to find it. To find you."

I didn't tell him that it wasn't me they were really searching for. I got the sense he wasn't crazy about the Zagrath, but I didn't know if this meant he was willing to hide a couple of fugitives. I took a tentative step toward a low chair.

He angled his head at me. "You are injured."

"In the crash, but it's nothing serious. Most likely a sprained ankle." I lowered myself gingerly into the chair, which I noticed was elaborately carved out of a deep-brown wood.

"And you walked all the way from your crashed ship to this village?" His gaze went to the door.

I drew in a long breath. "I had help."

He pursed his lips. "Zagrath."

"No, I'm telling you I have nothing to do with the empire. I'm actually trying to avoid being seen by them."

He straightened, taking his hands off the fabric he'd stretched across the table. "You are hiding from them?"

"You could say that."

He stared at me for a moment before taking a straight pin from a utility belt hidden by his jacket and pinning it to the fabric. "And your help?"

Moment of truth, I thought. Once I told him about Kaalek, there was no going back. Not that I had a lot of great options.

"He's a Vandar. The ship we crashed in was a Vandar ship, and we were trying to escape from a battle with the empire."

The Carlogian's brown eyes sharpened instantly. "The Vandar are here?"

"Only one," I said, "But he is a Raas."

The creature unpinned the fabric then pinned it again

absently, muttering to himself. "A Raas of the Vandar here on Carlogia Prime. I wonder..." His head snapped to me. "Where is he?"

"On the other side of this building, actually." I jerked a thumb at the wall Kaalek was no doubt still standing on the other side of. "He's in traditional Vandar attire, so we didn't think it was wise for him to walk into the village."

The small alien nodded. "Quite right, my dear." He dropped his voice. "The empire has spies everywhere."

"And you aren't a spy?" I asked, fixing him with my gaze. "You're not going to pretend to help us and then turn us over to the empire?"

His mouth fell open, then he clamped it shut. "I'm going to pretend you didn't just accuse me of conspiring with those responsible for taking over my planet."

"Plenty of planets have been occupied by the empire and a considerable number of the inhabitants have joined forces with the Zagrath, even turning in their own neighbors. How do I know you aren't one of those?"

His eyes filled, and his voice trembled. "Because they dragged my only son off to the mines, and I haven't seen him since. All you will find in this village are the ones who were not young enough or fit enough to do their backbreaking work. We have all lost children or mates to the mines. And none of us would lift a finger to help the empire."

Well, I felt like an asshole.

"I'm sorry," I whispered, the tears in his eyes making my own eyes sting.

He cleared his throat and looked down at the colorful fabric, folding it and placing another pin. "It is not your fault, human."

"You can call me Tara," I said. If I wasn't going to let Kaalek call me female, I wasn't about to let this little alien call me human.

He walked around the table and extended his hand. "I am Fenrey."

I shook his hand then inclined my head at his table and shelves. "It looks like you're a tailor."

He puffed out his chest. "The best tailor on Carlogia Prime."

Now that he was closer to me, I could see how perfectly his suit fit him, the seams invisible. "I believe you."

He allowed his gaze to moved down my body, although there was nothing predatory about it. "Do you mind if I ask what you're wearing, my dear?"

I'd almost forgotten that I was wearing a cobbled-together outfit grabbed from the Raas' quarters as we were leaving in a rush. "I had to borrow clothes from the Vandar. They don't allow females on their ships, so there wasn't much of a selection."

He wrinkled his squat nose. "I can see that." He spun on his heel and walked back to his table. "You can explain to me later how you ended up with the Vandar, if they do not take prisoners or allow females on their ships. First, I need to put you in something more appropriate. You won't ever look like one of us since your head is tragically hornless, but at least you can dress like us."

"That would be nice," I said. "But shouldn't we get Kaalek, so he doesn't get spotted by the Zagrath?"

He looked up briefly from his fingers fast at work. "Kaalek?"

"Sorry." Heat suffused my face. "That's the name of the Vandar Raas I'm with. Not that I'm *with* him in that way. Just that I'm here with him."

Fenrey smiled at me. "Of course, dear. Don't worry about your Vandar. I'm whipping up something for him, first."

My gaze went to the garishly patterned fabric that looked like shimmery velvet, and I grinned. This was going to be good.

CHAPTER FIFTEEN

Kaalek

I raked a hand through my hair. It was taking too long. Tara should have been back by now.

Glancing left and right, I sidled along the wall and peeked around the corner. The street was still deserted. Where were all the residents? Had the village been cleared out or evacuated? If so, where had Tara gone?

My stomach tightened. She hadn't used this chance to run from me, had she? Then I remembered her injured ankle. She wouldn't get far on that, not that I truly thought she would run. At this point, I didn't even think of myself as her captor, especially since I was planning to return her the first chance I got. But first, we needed to get off the planet and away from the empire.

A flash of color made me jump and reach for my axe as a creature came around the corner.

"Put this on," he said to me without preamble, tossing a pile of fabric at me, the texture velvety with a slight shimmer.

I fumbled to catch it since I was also trying to lift my axe. "What? Who—?"

The little alien with striped horns fluttered a hand at me. "You can ask me all the questions you want once you're safely inside my shop."

I stared at him, then down at the fabric. He was dressed in so many layers it was a wonder he didn't fall over from the heat, but no sweat beaded his burnished face. "But—"

"The human is with me, so please hurry." He swiveled his hand in the air. "I'd like to get her something more appropriate to wear before nightfall."

Since I wasn't going to get any more information from the unusually attired Carlogian, I unfurled the fabric and draped it over my shoulders. The garment had a hood, which I flipped up, pulling it low to cover my face as I followed the alien around the corner.

He opened the door and waved me through it, slipping in after me and closing the door with a resounding thunk. I immediately dropped the cloak from my shoulders, tossing it over a nearby chair. I kept my hand on the hilt of my axe as I scanned the small room. Tara stood behind a wooden table that dominated the space, looking up from a sketch and waving at me.

"Oh, good," she said. "You didn't try to kill Fenrey."

"He did reach for his weapon," the alien said, bustling by me to join her at the table. "But then he thought better of it." He tapped the paper she was looking at. "So, what do you think?"

"It's perfect." She fingered the edge of her leather vest. "As long as there's no leather, I'm thrilled." She peered up at me. "He's making us both outfits so we can blend in around here."

My gaze dropped to the Carlogian's elaborate clothing, and I put a hand instinctively to my throat. I couldn't imagine being covered by so much fabric.

"Do not worry, Vandar," the Carlogian named Fenrey said, the corner of his mouth quirking. "I have no intention of dressing you as stylishly as I am. Frankly, I don't have enough time, and I don't believe you could pull it off." His eyes widened as he gave me a once-over. "Not with your tail, and those ostentatious muscles."

I glanced down at myself. Ostentatious muscles?

As the two talked with their heads low, I swiveled to take in the small shop. After spending my life on a ship made of iron, the glow of the candlelight and the warm brown of the wood furnishings were a stark contrast. Since I was also used to vast cavernous spaces, the low, beamed ceiling was notable if not surprising. The Carlogian *was* barely half my height.

I took a breath, and my nose twitched. Did I smell food? My stomach growled in response, and I put a hand over it to muffle sound. Both Fenrey and Tara looked up.

"Lucky for you I put a nooseling in the oven a while ago." The Carlogian chuckled. "And also lucky for you, the nooseling is the biggest bird on our planet."

"Sounds delicious," Tara said.

The little alien disappeared through a set of heavy curtains into a back room, returning a few moments later with a tray holding a pitcher and goblets. "You both look like you need a little something now." He put the tray down on the table and nodded to me. "But especially you."

"What's all this about?" I asked, finally able to voice my confusion.

Tara gave me the smile you would give a child. "Fenrey agreed to help us, obviously. He's a tailor."

"The best tailor on the planet," the Carlogian added, pouring two goblets full of a clear liquid and handing one to Tara and one to me.

"Right," Tara grinned at him. "Not only is he the best tailor on the planet, but he's also part of the Carlogian resistance."

My ears perked up, as I took a long gulp of what tasted like water. It was so cool and crisp, I drained the goblet easily then set it down. "Carlogian resistance?"

The alien's expression became solemn. "Like I was telling Tara, the empire took everyone in our village who was strong enough or young enough to work in the mines. That doesn't mean those of us who are left aren't capable."

"I take it the Zagrath occupation was not welcome?" I asked, gratefully taking the goblet after he refilled it.

He frowned. "You of all people should know what it is like to have your planet taken over by those who only wish to strip it for *their* financial gain."

I lowered the goblet from my lips. "You know of the Vandar history?"

"I know why you do what you do, and why the empire works tirelessly to discredit you."

"How did I never know about this?" Tara threw her hands into the air. "All I ever heard was how terrifying and blood-thirsty the Vandar were."

I twitched one shoulder. "We are terrifying and bloodthirsty. If you stand with our enemy."

She folded her arms over her chest and shot me a look. If she was going to go into another longwinded explanation of why she was forced to work for the empire that had ruined so many lives, I did not want to hear it. It had not been long since I'd wanted to put her out an airlock, and making excuses for the Zagrath would bring all those homicidal feelings rushing back.

"So, what does this resistance do?" I asked.

Fenrey smiled, his wrinkled face losing much of its age. "We have found it most effective to perform small acts of sabotage. We do not have the brawn or weapons to stage a proper revolt, but we make life as difficult as possible for the imperial soldiers on the planet."

"Clever," I said. "It is just this village?"

He shook his head. "It's all over the planet. Each village or town has their own group, but we manage to get messages to each other with updates. All coded, of course."

As a Vandar Raas, I had liberated many outposts and colonies, but I had never encountered an underground network of resistance. It had never occurred to me to do anything but respond to the Zagrath with violence and fury. These aliens did not have warbirds and battle axes at their disposal, nor were they trained warriors. Yet still they resisted. The Carlogians impressed me.

"My horde was en route to assist in the liberation of your planet when we were attacked."

Fenrey blinked rapidly. "The Vandar are coming to help us?"

"We were," I admitted. "An attack by the empire forced us to regroup. The fe—Tara and I got separated and crashed on your planet. My horde does not know we are here, but they will figure it out soon enough. When they do, I would like for your resistance to be ready."

Fenrey set the pitcher down hard and some of the water sloshed out of the top. "I will send word to my network. We can increase our sabotage, so the empire is as weak and unprepared as possible when your horde arrives."

I inclined my head at him. "Just what I was thinking."

He disappeared through the curtain again, then poked his head back through. "Would you like to see?"

Tara exchanged a curious look with me, and we both followed him through the thick curtains and to the back of the shop. Since she was still hobbling, I picked her up without a word.

"If I don't, it will take us all night to get to what he wants to show us," I said, to preempt any complaints.

She had opened her mouth, but closed it and let me carry her.

The small room directly behind the front of the tailor's shop had a ceiling so low I had to bend my knees to keep from bumping my head. The walls were lined from floor to ceiling with mounted spools of thread in every color imaginable. The little alien continued walking, and we passed from the thread room into a kitchen.

The savory scent was more pronounced here, and the heat more intense. Fenrey rolled back a woven rug, put his finger in a knot in one of the floorboards, and pulled. The hatch was almost invisible to the eye and the hole had even been weathered to look like a true knot in the wood.

"Wow," Tara said, as I placed her feet gingerly on the floor, and we all peered down to a ladder that extended below the building. "You have a secret room."

"Not a room," Fenrey said, with pride in his voice. "A network of tunnels."

I nodded. "That is why your streets are deserted. You use the tunnels to move from building to building."

The Carlogian shrugged. "It avoids unwanted contact with the enemy. They think we are all old and lazy anyway, so they have never bothered to search our houses or shops after they first took our people. The sentries that were left in our village patrol a few times a day, and then sit in the public house and drink Carlogian ale."

"They drink on duty?" Tara asked, the disapproval clear on her face.

"It would normally not be enough to affect them since the Zagrath are larger than us, but the owner of the public house adds a little something extra for our guests."

"You drug them?" Tara grinned. "Nice."

"Fenrey!" The voice from below made us all jump, and I tightened my grip on the hilt of my weapon.

"Coxley?" Our Carlogian host peered into the darkness, then a light appeared, and a small face not unsimilar to Fenrey's was visible at the bottom of the ladder.

"It's me," the other Carlogian said, climbing up. "I came as soon as I could."

CHAPTER SIXTEEN

Tara

I guess I shouldn't have been surprised when the little guy popped out of the hole in the floor, but I was. Although he wasn't dressed quite as elaborately as Fenrey, he wore a tailored, blue coat over long pants and had a mass of dark curls that puffed up between his striped horns. His eyes were as large as his friend's, but his were an intense shade of blue.

Fenrey helped him out of the hatch and then closed it and rolled the rug back over. "Coxley, these are the two who crashed that ship."

Coxley's round eyes grew wider as he looked us both up and down. When he glanced at Kaalek, he made a small strangled noise in the back of his throat. "Did they, now?"

Fenrey rolled his eyes and prodded his friend forward. "This is Coxley. He's our village healer."

"Fenrey told me you'd been injured, so I came as quickly as I could." He held up a brown leather case.

"How did he tell you?" I asked before he could continue. "I've been with him the whole time."

Fenrey pivoted, lifting what looked like a breadbox on the nearby counter. Inside was a device with lots of keys, almost like one of those typewriters I'd seen a photo of in an ancient-history vid-book. "I sent him a quick message before I went out to get your friend."

I bent closer to the device, impressed with its simplicity and the fact that it wasn't computerized in any way. "And the empire can't track this?"

Fenrey shook his head, smiling widely. "It's only wires. Nothing they can detect."

The healer cleared his throat. "Should we go into the main room, so I can assess how badly you're hurt?"

Kaalek swooped me up in his arms again without asking and strode quickly through the small rooms until we'd reached the front of the shop. He put me down on a chair and stood behind it with his arms crossed and his tail swishing just above the floor. "She hurt her ankle in the crash."

The Carlogian healer nodded, his Adam's apple bobbing up and down as he took in the Raas standing guard over me. Kneeling down, he lifted my foot, his touch gentle.

Kaalek made a low noise in his throat, and Coxley almost dropped my foot, glancing up quickly.

"Ignore him," I said, smiling at the healer. I shot a look over my shoulder at the Raas. "Knock it off. He's trying to help."

Fenrey stood by the curtained doorway. "I'm going to check on the nooseling. It should be almost ready."

"Nooseling." Coxley sighed. "No one roasts a bird like Fenrey."

"You'll stay, of course," Fenrey called out, as he left the room for the back of the building.

The healer smiled, clearly pleased with the prospect of

dinner. He touched a finger to the puffy, blue bruise on my ankle that was becoming purple.

I flinched, Kaalek growled, and Coxley yelped.

I twisted to face the Raas. "Am I going to have to banish you to the kitchen?"

"Banish me?" A look of annoyed amusement crossed his face.

"Listen," I said. "I was here first. I made friends with Fenrey and convinced him to go bring you inside. We're guests here, so I suggest you stop growling at the healer who's trying to help me. It's not like I can spend the rest of my time on the planet being carried around by you."

He scowled down at me, but nodded.

Coxley let out an audible breath. "It's only a mild sprain, even though it looks bad. I'm going to rub some healing ointment on it to reduce the swelling and the pain. You should be able to walk on it again by morning."

"That fast?" I watched in fascination as he pulled a glass jar from his bag, turned the lid, and swirled his fingers in the orange goo.

"It's made from one of the medicinal trees in our forest. Quite powerful." He winked at me. "You never want to take this orally. You won't come down for days."

Kaalek shifted behind me, and Coxley dropped his eyes to my foot, clearing his throat as he rubbed a thick layer of the orange goo into my bruise until the color faded. My skin tingled where the ointment had been absorbed, warmth spreading up my leg.

"It's already working," I said. "The sharp pain is gone."

"Like I said, it's powerful." The healer tucked the jar back in his bag then pulled out a rag and wiped the ointment off his hands. "You'll be good as new tomorrow."

"Good," Kaalek said. "We need to be ready to run when my horde arrives."

"Horde?" Coxley's coppery skin lost a few shades.

"I didn't have time to tell you yet," Fenrey said, returning to the room with a platter that held an enormous, roasted bird with what appeared to be four wings instead of two. Ignoring the large worktable, he walked it to a smaller, round table off to the side. There was a single chair pulled up to it, and I suspected this was where the Carlogian ate his meals alone.

Coxley inhaled deeply as he stood. "You've outdone yourself, Fenrey."

The tailor preened slightly, as he twisted the platter to give the best view of the golden-brown bird surrounded by colorful, roasted cubes—what I assumed were some sort of root vegetables. "You know where I keep my plates, Coxley."

The healer bustled off to the back while Fenrey pulled up additional chairs, motioning for us to sit, which we did, the small chair groaning from Kaalek's weight. Coxley appeared again with four ceramic bowls and silverware, then Fenrey carved the nooseling with gusto, scooping rich broth over the meat and vegetables.

Even though we were crowded around the table, Kaalek's knee bumping mine, it was a pleasant meal. We were all so hungry, no one said a word until we'd nearly cleaned our plates, although I noticed Kaalek watching me handle my silverware before he picked up his.

"You were about to talk about the horde." Coxley dabbed at his mouth with his napkin, which was made with the same richly patterned, textured fabric as the curtains hanging across the back doorway.

"A Vandar horde is coming to help us overthrow the empire," Fenrey said, leaning forward and beaming at Kaalek. "And this is its Raas."

If Coxley's amber eyes could become any larger, they did at that moment. "A Raas? Here?" He dipped his head. "Your liege."

"Don't do that," I told Coxley, touching a hand to his arm. "He already has an enormous head."

"Of course, he does," the healer said earnestly. "A tiny head would look absurd on such a massive body."

I shook my head, ignoring Kaalek's broad smile. "I meant that he already thinks a lot of himself. Let's not encourage it."

Coxley looked like he might faint, and Fenrey looked as if he might burst into laughter. Kaalek, however, did not look amused. His smile had dropped.

"I only think highly of myself because I have fought hard and sacrificed much." His eyes snapped as he stared at me. "A Raas of the Vandar cannot afford false modesty. I know I'm a fierce warrior, and I have no shame in saying so."

I nudged Coxley, whose skin seemed slightly green. "See? I might be able to get behind the Vandar saving the world thing if they weren't so arrogant."

"Arrogant?" Kaalek squared his shoulders as if to intimidate me. Only the healer shrunk back in his seat.

Fenrey waved a hand to silence us both. "Do you hear that?"

Kaalek stopped arguing with me, but his glare did not falter. The Carlogian tailor leapt up from the table and hurried over to his window, pulling back the accordion shutter just enough to peek out. He put a hand to his heart.

"The imperial soldiers are back," he whispered, twisting to face us. "And they've brought what looks like part of a ship."

Kaalek rose, joining Fenrey at the window, a dark rumble escaping his throat when he looked out and the dark furry tip of his tail vibrating. "They have a section of our hull. The rest must have been too heavy to bring back." He straightened. "They now have evidence that a Vandar ship crashed nearby. They will be looking for me."

Fenrey straightened suddenly and jerked back from the window as if he'd been burned. "They're coming!"

Kaalek spun, his eyes dark and glittering. His hand went to the hilt of his battle axe.

"You can't kill the Zagrath soldiers," I said. "They'll know we're here." I saw his hesitation, and I glanced at our host. "It will put the Carlogians at risk."

Kaalek pressed his lips together and nodded. As much as he welcomed battle, he would not risk a village of people he'd come to save. "We will hide. For now."

Fenrey bustled across the room. "No time to get you below. Get in here." He pressed a wooden panel underneath the staircase that extended up the side of the room. The panel slid back, revealing a space large enough for a couple of Carlogians to fit.

I glanced at Kaalek then at the hiding place. "We can't fit in there."

A sharp rap on the door made us all jump. Fenrey waved furtively toward the space under the stairs, and Kaalek rushed to me, sweeping me up and carrying me with him.

I didn't have time to protest before he was ducking into the cramped space with me, and Fenrey was closing the panel behind us. The darkness was complete, and our bodies were pressed together as Kaalek crouched awkwardly, the only sound that of our breathing.

The walls were thicker than I'd expected. Even the sounds from the room were muffled, although it was clear when the door was opened to the Zagrath soldiers, the enemy voices sharper and louder than the Carlogian lilt.

"You have to stop doing that," I whispered.

"Doing what?" His mouth was so close to my ear he barely had to make any noise for me to hear him.

"Picking me up and carrying me."

He released a small sigh. "This again? I have no great desire to carry you. As soon as you have healed and can walk, I will be glad to let you—if only to cease your protests."

"Good."

He grunted then went silent as the voices in the room rose and fell. My heart hammered in my chest, and I braced myself for the door to fly open and blasters to be pointed at us. When that didn't happen and the voices faded, I let out a breath.

"Why are you doing this?" I asked after a moment.

"Doing what? You said I should not fight."

"Being nice to me," I whispered. "You were all set to force me to be your concubine or put me out an airlock and now...what?"

"I do not need to force any female. You would have been mine willingly."

I stifled a snort of laughter. "Don't count on it, Muscles. I'm not the type to fall into some guy's arms just because he's a warlord and has a big cock."

He was quiet for a beat. "Word of my cock has spread even to your sector?"

"Arrogant ass," I said under my breath, hating the amusement in his voice. I couldn't see him, but I knew he was smirking.

"If you must know, there are no airlocks here, and I am currently regretting not using the ones on my warbird," Kaalek said, "but make no mistake, Tara, you are still very much the property of the Vandar." His lips brushed my earlobe. "And I believe you *will* fall into my arms and enjoy every bit of my big cock."

Before I could tell him just how wrong he was, the door slid open. Fenrey and Coxley stared at us with wide eyes.

Kaalek stepped out first, pulling me by the hand behind him. "The soldiers are gone?"

"Fenrey convinced them we hadn't seen a thing." The healer grinned broadly at his friend.

Fenrey's expression wasn't as pleased. "They suspect a Vandar is in the village, but they have no proof. They only know your ship did not pilot itself, and there is a trail through the woods leading here."

I cringed. "I guess we weren't as stealthy as we thought we were."

"Don't worry." Fenrey patted me on the arm and headed for the curtained doorway. "I have a better place for you to hide. One that even if they search my shop, they won't find."

When none of us followed him, he paused and beckoned with his arm. "Come on, unless you want to be captured by the Zagrath." He fluttered a hand at the table we'd left. "As soon as you're hidden, Coxley and I will clean those off. The Zagrath didn't come inside just now, but they might be back, and I want no trace of you."

I was the first to follow the little alien back through the spool room—tiptoeing gingerly, although the pain in my ankle had already faded significantly—and into the kitchen, with Coxley and Kaalek bringing up the rear.

Fenrey rolled back the rug and opened the secret hatch, then began to back down the ladder. I peered into the dark hole and took a deep breath. Before I could start down, strong arms circled my waist and lifted me off the floor.

"Hey," I growled, as Kaalek tossed me over his shoulder. "What do you think you're doing?"

"You are still injured." He held my legs with one arm while holding onto the ladder with the other. "Would you prefer to fall down this hole?"

I rolled my eyes, but he couldn't see me as he descended the ladder. I still had a bone to pick with him about what he'd said while we were hiding, but I wouldn't do it in front of the nice villagers.

When we were all standing at the bottom of the ladder, Kaalek swung me down and Fenrey reached over and flicked a switch on the wall. Suddenly, strings of light hung high on the walls lit up the tunnel that stretched away from us in both directions.

I craned my neck to look down one side and then the other. Even though Kaalek had to bend slightly so that I didn't bump the ceiling, the tunnels were high enough for a Carlogian to walk easily and wide enough for them to walk at least two astride. "You weren't kidding about these tunnels. How did you make them so quickly?"

"The Zagrath have been here for over a standardized solar cycle," Coxley said, bitterness seeping from his voice.

"And we might have borrowed some of their mining equipment," Fenrey added.

Kaalek seemed impressed. "How long should we wait down here?"

"It would be safest if you two spent the night," Fenrey said.

I exchanged a glance with Kaalek. He looked as unhappy with that idea as I was. Probably more so, since the earthen ceiling was so close to his head.

"But not here," Coxley said, laughing. He walked forward and waved for us to join him. Kaalek made a motion to pick me up again, but I swatted him away and followed the Carlogian healer.

After a few steps, we reached an arched doorway cut into the tunnel. Coxley beamed as he stood on the threshold. "Fenrey has an emergency safe room." He lowered his voice. "In case he finds his son and can get him back, he would need to hide him from the empire."

Poking my head inside the room, I was surprised to see that it was a fully furnished bedroom with a wooden bed, nightstand and small desk. It looked cozy, if a bit small. "So, I'll stay here?"

Fenrey put a hand on my back. "You both will, dear. I only have one sleeping chamber above my shop."

Glancing back at the underground bedroom, I swallowed hard. There was only one bed—and it wasn't large.

CHAPTER SEVENTEEN

Kaalek

I stalked back and forth at the end of the bed. "I don't like this."

"Trust me, Muscles," Tara said from under the sheets. "I'm not crazy about it either."

I shot her a look then flicked a hand at the bed. "I don't mean this. I mean staying underground while the Zagrath walk around overhead."

Tara crossed her arms over her chest, which was now covered by a nightgown that the Carlogian tailor had whipped up for her, insisting that he couldn't go for one more minute, seeing her dressed in ill-fitting, battle garb. Like everything the little alien seemed to favor, it was richly colored—a mishmash of deep red, orange and yellow—but the fabric did look more comfortable for sleeping. He'd made a matching garment for me —something he called a nightshirt—but the enormous thing lay folded across the foot of the bed. Vandar did not wear clothes to sleep, and definitely not something that would bunch around our legs and make it difficult to fight if we were surprised in our slumber.

"What would you rather do?" she asked. "Run upstairs and burst out of Fenrey's front door? Take on all the Zagrath soldiers by yourself? Get captured, and get the aliens who helped us in trouble?"

I glared at her, hating that she was right. I couldn't risk the safety of the Carlogians who had helped us. I glanced around the room, the earthen walls glowing from the candle lamp on the side table. "I hate cowering down here."

Tara flopped back on the pillows. "We're not cowering." She popped back up. "Think of this like the invisibility shielding your ships use to sneak up on the enemy. These tunnels and this secret room are like that. They're keeping us hidden so we can take the imperial soldiers by surprise."

I held her gaze for a moment, hating how much sense she made. "When you were a captain, were you good at convincing your crew to do things they despised doing?"

She winked at me. "What do you think?"

I took a couple of long steps to my side of the bed and sat on the edge. "I think you are infuriating."

"Yep, that's what some of my crew thought, too."

"I am not surprised."

She laughed, clearly undeterred by my grumbling. "Listen, tough guy. I know it goes against every fiber of your Vandar heart to wait, but we need to be smart about this."

I whipped my head around to face her. "Are you saying I am not smart? I will have you know that I have planned the strategy for many—"

"I didn't say you aren't smart," she said, cutting off my complaints. "But your instinct to fight is probably at war with your brain right now."

I growled, despising how right she was.

"All I'm saying is that there's more at stake now. These

Carlogians are going out on a limb to harbor us from the empire. We can't repay them by being rash, or by getting caught. If you really want to beat the empire as much as you say you do, then you'll take a fucking breath and work with me to come up with a plan."

I narrowed my eyes at her. "Work with you to come up with a plan? You seem to have forgotten that you are my captive, Tara."

She tilted her head at me, her green eyes also narrowing. "After all this, you still think I'm some sort of prisoner?"

Even though my intention was to return her to her ship, I was not going to tell her that. Not when she was so busy trying to flex her captain muscles. Besides, I enjoyed sparring with her. If I could not rush out and strike down the Zagrath, arguing with her would provide some enjoyment. I leaned over so that our faces were nearly touching. "I remember you agreeing to be my prisoner."

She drew in a sharp breath and pulled back. "That's not how I remember it. I agreed to go with you to your ship. We're not on your ship anymore."

I shook my head, making a *tsk*-ing noise at her. "If I remember correctly, you said you'd do anything if I agreed not to blow up your ship. I kept my end of the bargain, but it seems you are the dishonorable one who won't keep hers."

She pursed her lips. "I went with you to your ship. I let you tie me up. I came with you on this disaster of a mission. What more do you want?"

I cocked an eyebrow at her. "You did not *agree* to be tied up. My *majak* had to tie you because you were dangerous—and you gave him the scar to prove it. Then you tried to kill me."

"You really can't let that one go, can you? If it makes you feel better, you're not the first guy I've tried to kill."

"Yes," I said, my tone flat. "That makes me feel much better.

I'm sleeping with a female who has tried to kill me and many other males."

Her cheeks reddened. "We're not sleeping together. We're just sleeping in the same bed. And all I was saying is that you shouldn't take it personally."

"I will keep that in mind." I stood and unfastened one of my chest straps. "As long as you remember that you have not yet fulfilled your promise to me."

I dropped first one leather and metal strap to the floor and then another, finally unhooking my shoulder armor and letting the scaled caps fall. I kicked off my boots, then I removed my battle axe and propped it against the wall—within easy reach if we were surprised in the night. When I started to take off my kilt, Tara inhaled sharply.

"What are you doing?"

I twisted my head to see her wide eyes taking me in. "I am undressing for bed."

She pointed to the nightshirt Fenrey had left for me. "Don't you need that?"

I laughed and slid my battle kilt down bit more. "Vandar do not sleep in dresses."

"Well, you can't sleep naked."

I eyed her and the pink flush crawling up her neck. I had heard that humans were not as open with nudity or as free with their bodies, but Tara had not struck me as a typical human female. "You do not trust me to sleep unclothed next to you?"

Now she barked out a laugh. "Not by a long shot, Muscles."

I frowned. "If you continue to call me Muscles, I will have to go back to calling you female."

"Fine," she huffed out. "I don't trust you."

I growled low, dropping my kilt to the floor. "It has been a long day. I discovered my horde had been tracked by the empire, we were separated from them and shot, we crashed onto an alien planet, you were injured due to your stubbornness, I carried you through a forest, and now we are hiding in a secret tunnel. I have no intention of doing anything but sleeping, Tara."

Her eyes were fixed on mine, but I could tell she was trying hard not to stare at what was hanging long between my legs. "Do you promise?"

I let out an impatient sigh. "You and your promises. Fine." I leaned over and put my arms on the bed. "I will promise not to fuck you tonight if you will admit that you are still my captive."

The pink in her cheeks deepened. "I should kick you in the balls."

I flicked my gaze at her legs pinned under the blanket. "I would like to see you try."

She held my eyes for a moment longer, then looked away. "Okay, fine." She waved a hand in the air. "I'm your captive. Whatever. As long as you keep that…" She pointed to my cock without looking at it. "…on your side of the bed."

I pulled back the blanket and slipped under it. "I will try, but as you pointed out before, it is big."

She muttered to herself, as she leaned over and extinguished the lamp, then turned pointedly away from me, scooting to the edge of the bed.

As much as the female frustrated me, she also amused me. And she had been right about waiting. If we came up with a sound strategy, we could make the Vandar incursion more successful, and ensure that the empire left the Carlogians to govern themselves. That was what I wanted, after all. To repel the empire and make another chink in their armor. Thinking about battling the empire made my heart beat faster.

I glanced at the lump in the bed next to me. I also wanted nothing more than to roll on top of the female and spread her legs. Even the thought made me harden, my swollen cock making a large bump under the blanket. I raised my arms and put them behind my head, trying to focus on anything but the warm female next to me. Why had I promised not to touch her when it was the only thing I wanted to do?

Take her, a little voice in my head told me. *You are a Raas of the Vandar, and she is your captive. She is yours to claim.*

Tvek. The voice—hard and relentless—sounded like my father, like it always did. At least, what I remembered of my father. And, like always, his voice was the last one I wanted to hear judging me and finding me lacking. I pushed the voice away, telling myself that I was not my father. I was better than him—more feared and more ruthless. He might have left me behind to go raiding with my older brother, but I had not needed him to become a Raas who was feared throughout the sector. A Raas who was ruthless and took without asking.

Then take her like you take everything, a voice that was not my father insisted.

I fisted my hands. As much as I wanted to bury my cock inside her as she begged for more, I could not break my promise. A Vandar Raas did not lie.

A Raas also did not make promises to human prisoners. But I had now made several, and I was not willing to break them.

I shifted in bed and tried to ignore my cock, instead reliving glorious battles in my head in hopes that memories of blood and death would dampen my desire for the aggravating female.

CHAPTER EIGHTEEN

Tara

I woke to something heavy flopping across my stomach. What the hell? I opened my eyes, but it was pitch dark. For a moment I forgot where I was, my mind putting me back on my freighter. But the freighter was never so dark or so quiet. On a spaceship, there was always the low rumbling of the engines, the clattering of a pipe, or the sounds of someone walking across the steel floors. There was never silence like this that surrounded me like a shroud.

It took me a few seconds to remember that I was underground in a secret room beneath the Carlogian tailor's shop. It took me a few more beats to remember that Kaalek was asleep beside me. Well, not totally asleep. I couldn't see him, but I could feel him thrashing beside me.

I pushed his arm off me and exhaled gratefully once the heavy thing wasn't pressing on my stomach. Almost as soon as I did, his thrashing got more intense, and he started to mutter urgently in his sleep.

"Take me with you." His voice was so pained I almost couldn't recognize it. If I hadn't seen him—all of him—crawling into bed next to me, I never would have believed such an agonized tone could be his.

"Kaalek," I whispered. I knew he was dreaming, but he also sounded like he was in a lot of pain.

"Don't leave me!" His voice rose to a near-shriek, but it also sounded child-like.

I shook him lightly, but he only thrashed more, his arms and feet flailing. Whatever dream he was having, it wasn't good. After seeing how tough the Raas was, it was hard to imagine him suffering from nightmares, but everyone held secrets and pain. Just because he was a warlord didn't make him immune from either.

He stopped moving, and I exhaled a breath. Then he let out a wail that made the hair on the back of my neck stand up.

I had to break him out of the dream. Shaking his shoulder harder, I whispered, "It's okay, Kaalek. You're dreaming."

The wailing stopping, replaced by a low growl that made me freeze.

"I'll show you." Now this was the voice I knew—hard and driving. "I'll make you sorry."

I lifted my hand carefully from his shoulder, but before I could pull it back, he'd grabbed it and rolled me back, with him on top. His hard body pressed flush against mine, so heavy it made it hard for me to take a breath. He quickly nudged my knees apart, his cock hardening between my thighs and his tail stroking up and down the sides of my body that were not covered by his own. He still held one wrist in his hand, and had it pinned over my head. With the other, I slapped him as hard as I could.

"Get off me!" I tried to push him off, but he was too heavy.

His face was only inches from mine, and his breath was warm and fast on my cheek. He shifted between my thighs, the rigid bar of his cock sliding easily in my wetness. Then his tail tickled the inside of my thigh, and I almost whimpered.

Fuck. Now is not the time to get turned on, Tara.

"Kaalek!" I screamed. "Wake up!"

He jerked and then stilled. It seemed to take him a minute to determine he wasn't wherever he'd thought he was, then he sagged against me, burying his head in my neck as he shook.

Even though he'd stopped moving his cock, it was still notched at my slick opening. My cheeks flamed at my body's traitorous response to him being on top of me—my nipples were hard against his chest, and I was practically panting. It didn't help that all I could think about was the fact that I'd seen how huge his cock was, and that it was covered with the same swirling marks that curled across his chest.

"Kaalek," I said, trying my best to steady my voice. "Can you get off me?"

His arms stiffened, and he rolled off me. "What...what happened?"

I reached for the side table and fumbled for the lamp, my hand shaking as I lit it. Warm light suffused the room, and I dragged the blanket up around my chest before I turned to face him. "You had a nightmare."

He sat up so that his back was propped against the wooden headboard, which he dwarfed. "A nightmare? Impossible. I don't dream."

"Everyone dreams," I said gently, "even if you don't remember it."

He frowned. "I must have been remembering a violent battle." He glanced over at me. "Did I hurt you?"

"No," I told him. "But you weren't dreaming about a battle. You were really angry at someone. Someone who left you."

His face paled, pain evident behind his eyes, then something shifted in him, and he shook his head. "I am only angry at the empire. They are my only enemy."

His words sounded so automatic—so rehearsed—that I had to stifle a laugh. Who was he kidding? I looked at his stormy expression and the white line of his mouth. I guess he was fooling himself.

As huge and terrifying as he was when he was in a fury, it was hard for me to be scared of him when I'd gotten a glimpse of the pain he held inside himself.

"Listen," I said. "I get it. I didn't want to admit to my crew how devastated I was when Astrid left. I was the captain, so I couldn't let them see how hurt I was that she'd let herself be taken as a captive, even if it was to save me. I cried myself to sleep for days after she was taken."

His eyes betrayed no emotion. "There is no one I would cry over."

"Well, that's pretty sad."

"I am not like you, human. I am Vandar. I was raised to be a raider and a Raas. There is no room for attachment or tears in my world."

I studied him, his dark hair hanging wild around his face, his eyes rimmed with red. He'd probably suppressed the pain so deeply that it only came out in his dreams—bits of his true self slipping out under the cover of darkness.

I decided not to push him. Not now. I changed my tone and gave him a sly smile. "Are you telling me you wouldn't cry over me?"

He choked back a laugh. "I would only cry if I learned I would be stuck here forever with you."

I made a face at him. "You wish, Muscles."

The corner of his mouth twitched slightly. "I promise you, I do not, female."

I gave him a reluctant smile, then I tugged the blanket

higher, darting a glance at the outline of his cock. "Now if I go back to sleep again, do you think you can promise not to molest me again?"

"That would imply that my attentions were completely unwanted." He lifted the blanket and peeked under at himself. "And my cock is still soaked with your juices."

I sucked in a breath, as heat made the skin on my chest prickle. "Yeah, well, you weren't supposed to have your huge thing anywhere close to my...juices." I cringed at the word and at the fact that his smile had broadened as soon as I'd called his cock huge. "You were supposed to stay on your side."

He shrugged, as if he was unconcerned by the fact that he'd nearly sleepfucked me. "It is hard to stick to one side when the bed is so small. When I sleep with a female, I'm used to her being next to me or on top of me."

"I think you've probably figured out by now that I'm not one of your usual females." I used air quotes on the last two words.

"Unfortunately." He sighed and slipped under the blanket. "But it is your loss."

"Doubtful," I mumbled as I leaned over and once again extinguished the light. "I'll bet my ass you're too fast a draw for my taste."

I settled back down under the covers, flouncing over on my side to face away from him. Just as I was thinking how infuriating the alien was, he was rolling over so that his mouth was by my ear.

"If by fast draw, you mean that I would come before you are satisfied, then you are wrong. I am quite skilled at pleasuring females, and I would never stop fucking you until your screams of pleasure filled my ears."

As quickly as he'd rolled over to me, he rolled away, leaving my skin scorched from where his lips had touched it and leaving my body tingling. I hadn't even come up with a decent response when the rhythmic breathing of his sleep gave way to soft snoring. That asshole had actually fallen asleep.

I turned over and lay on my back, my body burning with arousal as I thought of all the ways I could kill Kaalek and get away with it.

CHAPTER NINETEEN

Kaalek

Even though there was no light to wake me, my body roused me at what I suspected was my usual waking time. I blinked, absorbing the darkness and the fact that I was curled up against something soft.

Tara. Her body was tucked inside the curve of my larger one, her ass pressed into my abdomen. I gritted my teeth and willed my cock not to rise, although it was already swelling. My tail, which draped over the gentle rise of her hip, twitched with arousal. I moved it off her body and behind mine.

I didn't know how we ended up sleeping body-to-body, but I suspected she would not be pleased to wake and find me on her again, even if this time I was only lying on my side with her next to me. And soon my cock would be rock-hard and poking her legs.

I rolled away slowly, then realized one of my arms was

pinned underneath her. *Tvek!* As I tried to extricate myself, lights came on in the tunnel and illuminated the room.

"Greetings of the day," Fenrey said merrily, as he walked in carrying a tray.

I yanked my arm hard, sending Tara spinning off the bed and onto the floor.

"Son of a bitch!" she cried, pulling herself up by the edge of the bed and glaring at me. "Did you push me?"

"It looked like you just rolled right off," the Carlogian said, before I could defend myself. He set the tray at the foot of the bed and hurried over to her. "Let me help you up, dear."

Tara rubbed her elbows as she stood, still giving me a side-eye glance. "Lucky for you I didn't break my arm."

Fenrey reached over and lifted her gown slightly. "And your ankle looks healed."

I followed his gaze and saw that he was right. Tara's ankle, which had been swollen and purple the day before, looked almost normal. I would have to talk to that Coxley fellow about his ointment. Something that healed wounds so quickly would be an asset on a Vandar warbird.

"It feels like nothing ever happened to it," Tara admitted, swiveling her foot in the air.

Fenrey bobbed his head up and down. "You won't find a healer as skilled as Coxley." His gaze moved up from her foot, his eyes shrewd. "Well the gown certainly suits." He put his hand up to his mouth and pretended to talk to her behind it. "Much better than that absurd ensemble you had on yesterday." Then he glanced at me and the nightshirt draped over the foot of the bed. "I see others prefer to be au naturel."

Despite my ease at being naked, warmth tinged my cheeks.

"It's all right." He fluttered a hand at me. "Not everyone prefers sleeping clothes, but don't worry. I have quite the outfit for you today."

I gazed longingly at my battle kilt, but knew he was right.

Even though I wouldn't easily fit in among the Carlogians, my Vandar clothing would make it impossible. "I look forward to trying it on."

He rubbed his hands. "Excellent." He nodded to the tray. "I brought you tea and Carlogian biscuits. Have a nibble, and I'll go get the clothes I've been working on."

"You must like to work early," Tara said, picking up one of the steaming handleless cups and taking a sip.

"Early?" Fenrey let out a laugh. "It's already mid-morn. I let you sleep because I was sure you'd be exhausted after the day you had yesterday, and I was right. At least you both look better than you did last night, when you were nearly dead on your feet."

"Mid-morn?" I sat up. "You mean we slept late?"

He looked unruffled. "I don't know what sleeping late is to you, but I've been up and about for hours, which gave me time to finish your garments." He flapped a hand at us again. "Eat your breakfast while I run up."

And with that, he disappeared back down the tunnel.

Tara picked up one of the Carlogian biscuits and nibbled at it. "Not bad. Unusual spices, but tasty."

Even though we'd eaten the night before, my stomach rumbled as I took a bite of the other diamond-shaped bread. Tara was right. Not bad, and a little like Vandar sweet bread. I finished it in a few bites and washed it down with the strong tea, which tasted faintly of grass.

I swung my feet over the side of the bed to stand up then remembered that I wasn't dressed. I didn't mind Tara seeing me, but I thought a naked Vandar might be too much for Fenrey. At that moment, he bustled back in, his eyes fortunately on the bundles of clothes in both hands.

"For the lady, I put together something practical, yet flattering." He handed some folded cloth to Tara. "And for the raider, I went with something to help him blend in."

I examined the fabric he handed me. It was black, which was surprising, since I'd only seen colorful, patterned fabrics in his shop. I unfurled it to find that it was a pair of long pants and a matching tunic that closed in the front with a pair of loops.

"Go on and get dressed," the tailor said, backing out of the room. "Then join us upstairs."

"Thanks, Fenrey," Tara called out, then turned to me. "Wait, did he say 'us?'"

"He did." I slipped my feet through the pants then stood up to tug them on as Tara jerked her gaze away from me. The fabric seemed to mold itself to my skin—even with a flap for my tail—and I was amazed by how perfectly the Carlogian had sized me up just by sight. I shrugged on the tunic, which fell to my knees and showed a sliver of bare chest, since it did not close fully in front. Even though the sleeves were long, the fabric stretched as I moved, so I could wave my arms overhead without splitting it. Fenrey truly was skilled at his profession.

"Damn," Tara said from behind me. "He really nailed you, didn't he?"

I twisted to answer and stopped with my mouth open. She'd exchanged her shapeless nightgown for a pair of pants as form-fitting as mine—but hers were a forest-green—and on top she wore a golden-brown sleeveless top that showed a slice of bare midriff and was embellished along the edges in shimmering thread. I finally recovered myself and frowned.

"What?" She put her hands on her hips. "Is it the tight pants again? I promise you none of these Carlogians are going to be staring at my ass."

"I suppose you're right, but did he have to show so much flesh?"

She threw her head back and laughed. "Says the guy who sleeps in the buff and had no problem flashing me last night."

"That is different," I said.

Her eyes flashed in challenge. "Why? Because you're a guy?"

"No." I walked around the bed and put a hand on her waist. "Because you are still my...responsibility."

She pursed her lips and pulled them to one side. "You were really close to saying I was your property and getting kneed in the balls."

I instinctively placed my hand over my crotch. "I did not say property."

"Good, because I may have agreed to come on your ship to save my freighter, but that doesn't mean I belong to you."

I used my hand on her waist to pull her closer. "You know, there might come a time when you wish for the protection of a Raas."

She peered up and met my gaze, letting out a shuddering breath. "Today is not that day." She stepped back and out of my grip. "Now I'm going upstairs to find out who Fenrey meant when he said *us*."

CHAPTER TWENTY

Tara

"I did not expect *this*." I hesitated, after pushing through the curtain divider into the front of the shop. Instead of being greeted by Fenrey, we were met by half a dozen pairs of wide eyes.

Kaalek almost walked into me, as I stopped short and smiled uneasily at the Carlogians sitting on wooden chairs or standing around the large worktable. Like the tailor, they were all short, with nut-brown skin and colorful, striped horns. And like him, they wore clothing that consisted of many layers and often contrasting patterns.

"Come, come." Fenrey spun around and waved us forward. "We were just discussing the plan to overthrow the empire."

A female Carlogian with dark hair flowing long between her horns offered us cups of tea, but Kaalek and I both declined. Her gaze lingered on the Vandar, her pupils flaring as she clearly sized him up. She made a tiny squeak in the back of her throat and scurried back around the table.

Even though the Zagrath soldiers were taller than the Carlogian natives, they still didn't compare to the Vandar in height or sheer muscle mass. And in the black outfit Fenrey had made for him, Kaalek looked pretty menacing.

"What is your plan?" Kaalek asked, clasping his hands behind him.

A nervous laugh escaped Fenrey's lips. "We don't have one yet."

"We were discussing the fact that we *should* have one," Coxley added, smiling eagerly from his chair by the small round table we'd dined at the night before.

"That's a first step, I guess," I said under my breath to Kaalek when I saw the startled expression on his face. "They aren't Vandar like you. They don't live and breathe battle."

He made a grunting sound of disapproval, scanning the small group. If he saw what I did, I could imagine that he wasn't thrilled. I'd remembered that Fenrey had told us that most of the able-bodied and young had been taken to the mines, but the few villagers in his front room did not look like fighters. There was only one other female, the one who'd offered us tea, and one gray-haired Carlogian sitting down with both of his hands resting on top of a cane. Another two villagers had almost as many wrinkles as our host, and a particularly skinny alien with russet hair like a tuft of steel wool scratched nervously at his arms. If this was the resistance, we could be in trouble.

Fenrey cleared his throat. "We might not look like much to a Raas of the Vandar, but don't underestimate the heart of a Carlogian." He walked around the table and put a hand on the shoulder of one of the older males. "Rix here is our village chemist. When we were boys we used to love to blow things up."

"Still do," Rix said, tugging on one of his oversized ears. "Just haven't done it in a while."

"An explosives man." Kaalek nodded at him solemnly. "Do you have enough supplies, or did the empire clean you out?"

The Carlogian chemist grinned. "I still run a chemist shop across the way, and supply medicine to everyone in the village. They didn't dare shut me down. Not when I give them free health elixirs."

I cocked my head at him. "Are they really health elixirs?"

His grin widened. "Professional secret."

"Rix supplies all the sleeping draughts we give to the soldiers when they're at the public house," Coxley said, with a certain amount of pride in his voice.

"We have a chemist who can drug soldiers and make explosives." Kaalek rocked back on his heels. "That's a good start."

The Carlogian with the cane tapped it sharply on the floor. "I'm the engineer who built the water system for the village. If you need anything mechanical built, I can tell you how to do it," He raised a gnarled hand. "even if my hands can't do the work anymore."

"And I can make anything you need out of wood." The skinny Carlogian said, rubbing his palms on the front of his pants.

"Taiko is a master carpenter," Fenrey said, then dropped his voice. "Lucky for us, his nerves didn't make him a good candidate for the mines."

The villagers stared hopefully at Kaalek, and I nudged him. "Well, what do you think?"

He inclined his head at them. "I think the empire has once again underestimated the people they are trying to conquer."

"Do you think we can do it?" Coxley asked, bouncing one leg up and down.

"Our objective should be to create a distraction when my horde arrives," Kaalek said. "We want the imperial soldiers to be so confused they won't be able to mount a defense or call for additional forces."

"How do we know when your horde will arrive?" Fenrey asked.

"We don't," the Raas shifted from one foot to the other. "Which means we have to be ready as soon as possible. If I know my crew like I do, they will not delay in searching for my ship, and it will not take them long to track it down. Even if the Zagrath found my ship and deactivated my homing beacon."

"We're ready." Fenrey rubbed his small hands together.

"Do you have a map of the village and the surrounding area?" Kaalek asked.

"I brought one," one of the elder Carlogians said, pulling a roll of yellowed paper from a leather satchel. He walked it over to the worktable, unrolling it as he went. Stretching it flat across the surface, he used his arms to hold down the sides. Kaalek and I joined him, and the other villagers gathered around.

"We're here." Fenrey pointed to a square indicating his shop at the edge of the village. He then pointed out the other shops— the chemist shop, the carpenter's woodshed, the bakery, and the public house.

It was curious to watch Kaalek with his head bent over the map surrounded by the diminutive aliens. Mostly what I'd seen of him was what I'd expected from a Vandar—fighting and threats and action—but this was a different side of him. It made sense that a warlord would be no stranger to strategy, but as I eyed him studying the map and listening carefully to the Carlogians, it hit me that he was not exactly what I'd expected. It was almost unsettling to discover how wrong my initial assumptions had been, and it was very unnerving that this more civilized side of Kaalek made it harder to dislike him.

When he swiveled his head to look at me—one eyebrow raised—I realized I'd been staring. I cleared my throat and said the first thing that came to my mind. "Are all of the buildings in the village connected underground?"

"Not all," Coxley said, and he and Fenrey exchanged a nervous glance. "There are a few villagers who sympathized with the empire, or have refused to become part of the resistance."

There were dark mumbles and frowns from everyone.

"I give them the over-salted bread only," the female Carlogian said, and I assumed she was the village baker.

More nods of approval.

"Will the traitors cause any trouble?" Kaalek asked. "Do we need to eliminate them?"

I dug an elbow into his ribs as the Carlogians gaped at him. "We're not going to off a bunch of their neighbors just because they're not on our side."

He scowled and his eyebrows pressed together. "Why not? If they are willing to sell out their people to the empire, they deserve death."

There was that Vandar impulse again. I noticed the carpenter's dark skin lose a few shades of color. "Because they aren't Vandar, and not everyone executes people for disagreeing with them."

He let out a frustrated sigh and turned back to the villagers. "If you do not wish to take them out, we will need to ensure that they are unable to warn the enemy."

"I can give them something that will keep them occupied by violent retching for at least one full solar rotation," the chemist said. "Or a powerful sleeping draught."

"And I will make sure not to give them the right cure," Coxley added, waving a finger in the air.

"That takes care of the possible informers," Kaalek said. "Now where is the nearest mine in relation to this map?"

The frail engineer tapped a finger on the top corner of the map. "Right about here. Half a day's walk."

Kaalek drummed his fingers on the table, clearly in thought. "I would like to destroy the mines, so the empire has little incentive to return. As long as there is something of value on this planet, they will keep coming for it, but they will tire of rebuilding mines."

"And we can't destroy a mine if these people's children and friends are down inside it," I reminded him.

He cut his eyes to me. "We would have to get them out first. Even then, the empire would only dig another."

"Then maybe instead of destroying it, we liberate it and put the Carlogians in charge?" I suggested. "The rare minerals are from their planet. Why shouldn't they mine them and sell them?"

The baker shook her head. "The empire would never allow it."

"They would if they thought you were protected by the Vandar," I said. "An entire horde of Vandar."

Kaalek quirked an eyebrow at me. "My horde could expel the Zagrath, but we have never stayed as sentry guards for a planet."

"Maybe you don't have to stay forever, as long as the enemy thinks you're here."

"And why would they think that?" Kaalek folded his massive arms across his chest and peered down at me.

"A trick, an illusion, like the trick you play to hide your ships." I gave him a pointed look. "I don't know all the details. I can't come up with everything, but I'm sure it's possible. Besides, I know the Vandar are good with technology. Can't you figure it out?"

He opened his mouth, and I could tell that he was going to argue. Then he stopped, tapped a finger on his jaw and the corner of his mouth quivered. "I still believe we should blow up the mines, but you might be onto something, female."

"I'm glad you think so, Muscles."

CHAPTER TWENTY-ONE

Kaalek

It took us most of the day—and many cups of Carlogian tea and baskets upon baskets of freshly baked bread courtesy of the village baker, who kept dashing back and forth from Fenrey's shop to her bakery through the tunnels—but we devised a plan to distract the imperial soldiers stationed on the planet.

Many times, I caught Tara looking intently at me, as if she was trying to figure something out, but then she would flush and turn away or ask Fenrey a question. She'd told me over and over that she did not want me, yet her gaze said otherwise. But I did not have time to focus on the maddening nature of human females. Not when there was a revolt to plan.

I leaned over the table, my hands braced wide. "Let's go over it again."

"First, we take out the villagers who aren't with the resistance," Rix, the chemist said, adding quickly. "But not permanently."

I nodded, although if it had been entirely up to me I would have eliminated any threat. In my experience, those who were willing to sell out their neighbors could never be trusted. But Tara was right that not everyone was as willing to make tough decisions that were part and parcel of being a Vandar raider, and especially a Raas. Sentimentality was something I'd abandoned long ago.

"Then we set up trip wires underneath the main village street," the old engineer said, his shaky voice strong as he talked about his part in the plan. "When the imperial soldiers run through, it will set off a series of explosions."

"And you can set these explosions so they won't cave in our tunnels, Brylynn?" Fenrey asked, glancing back at the doorway leading to his secret tunnel.

The old Carlogian gave a brusque nod. "Of course."

"But I'll shore up the tunnels with beams, just to reinforce the ceilings," Taiko, the carpenter, said. He'd stopped nervously scratching his arms the more we'd talked about his part in the plan, especially when he'd explained which trees in the forest would be best for the job.

"And I'll supply the chemicals to Brylynn," Rix added. "And help him with the construction."

"That takes care of the soldiers who come through the village," Tara said as she returned from the back room with more paper. "What about the rest of them?"

Coxley, took it from her eagerly and spread a clean sheet across the table. "While the imperial soldiers posted to this village are being neutralized," he cringed at the word, "we send our fastest runners to the mines."

I straightened. "That would be me."

"Well, you're not going without me," Tara said.

I looked down at her, as she stood with her hands on her hips. "Don't be foolish. Yesterday, you could barely walk. Now you wish to run for hours?"

"Her ankle should be healed enough to support her, even on a long run," Coxley said. "I reapplied the ointment earlier, when you were discussing the blasting points on the road."

I cut my eyes to him. "Do not encourage her."

He made a strangled sound before shrinking back into his chair.

"See?" Tara swept her arm wide to point at Coxley. "Even the healer says it's fine. I'm not saying I'm excited about it, but you need a wingman, and who else is going to do it?"

I didn't need to assess the Carlogians in the room to know that none of them would be able to keep up with me. Some of them couldn't even walk. That didn't mean I needed to put Tara at risk, though. There was a chance that the imperial soldiers in the village might get off a transmission before we could eliminate them all, so we could be running toward a mine with a full complement of fighters who were ready for an attack.

I shook my head and turned back to the worktable and our diagrams. "Out of the question."

All the Carlogians shifted and a few took a step away from me.

"Excuse me?" She pulled my arm to pivot me back to her. "Who said you get to decide what I can or can't do?"

An uncomfortable ripple of muttering passed through the room, and all eyes were on me.

I stifled a groan. "Are all human females as difficult as you *all* the time? If so, I am amazed my brother's horde has survived your sister for as long as it has."

Her jaw tensed. "Astrid isn't like me, so I'm sure your brother's horde is just fine. She probably didn't even *attempt* to kill him."

"Imagine that," I said.

Her green eyes sparked as she narrowed them at me. "You shouldn't bring up my sister if you want my help."

"I do not want your help. Not in this way. It is too dangerous."

"Listen, buddy." She jabbed a finger at my chest and someone in the room sucked in air. "I was the captain of my own ship. I've outsmarted Vandar raiders before. Danger doesn't scare me."

I tried to ignore the physical jab and the jab at my horde. "You only think you outsmarted me, Tara. I knew very well what you were hiding on your ship."

Her mouth fell open, then she clamped it shut. "I don't believe you."

I closed the distance between us and lowered my head so that I could whisper in her ear. "You don't think I knew your crew was hidden on your ship just waiting for us to leave?"

The female's sharp inhalation of breath betrayed her. "Then why did you let them go?"

"Leverage." I put a hand on her waist, slipping my fingers underneath the fabric of the cropped top. "So, I could get what I wanted."

She reared back. "It was your plan all along to take me onto your ship?"

"Not all along," I admitted. "The plan solidified when I saw you standing half-naked in your room."

"Typical Vandar," she said, her voice dark.

My gaze locked on hers. "If I was a typical Vandar, I would have claimed you already when you were tied to my bed."

Coxley sat down hard on a chair, a small squeak escaping his lips.

Fenrey cleared his throat. "Now might be a good time for a break."

"Yes." Coxley stood, his gaze darting around the room at anything but me or Tara. "Maybe we should adjourn for middies, and come back later to finish reviewing the plan?"

I didn't know what 'middies' was but I guessed it was a meal of some kind. The Carlogians seemed to like lots of meals throughout the day.

Tara wasn't dissuaded. She held my gaze then folded her arms over her chest. "None of that is going to make me change my mind. I'm not sitting this one out, so you can either accept that I'm going with you, or prepare yourself to be chased the entire way."

I turned away from her, cursing the day I'd decided to spare her ship and her crew and take her as my captive. I had not been expecting to form mating marks with her, but I'd hoped for a few nights with her underneath me. Not only had she *not* been a pleasant diversion, my balls were so blue I suspected they might fall off. Verbal sparring with her was all well and good, but now she was threatening to ruin my plan to bring down the imperial hold on Carlogia with her stubbornness.

The villagers muttered farewells as they left the front room, passing through the curtained doorway and exiting through the tunnel. When the room had emptied—Fenrey's muffled voice wishing all his guests well from the back of the shop—Tara stomped around the table to face me.

"You do know we're in this together, right?"

"If you mean we crashed on this planet together, then yes."

She threw her hands in the air. "I mean, that I care just as much as you do about this plan and defeating the empire. I want the soldiers off Carlogia, too. And to make that happen, you need to let me be a part of the plan."

I looked at the fiery curls spilling down her shoulders and the pink splotches on her cheeks. Thinking of her running toward danger with me made my stomach twist into a hard ball.

Tvek. Why did I care about a female who had been nothing but trouble? I should let her come with me and risk her life. If she was killed, she would be one less thing for me to worry about. But I knew I couldn't. The thought of her being hurt again made the hard ball of fear in my gut churn. Having her by my side would only be a distraction that would make me a weak warrior. I could not battle the Zagrath if I was worried about her safety.

"I have made my decision." I shook my head at her. "It is done."

CHAPTER TWENTY-TWO

Tara

"That arrogant asshole." I jumped the last rung of the ladder and landed on the packed ground. I was pleased that my ankle had made a full—and miraculously quick, thanks to Coxley's ointment—recovery, but it was another reminder that Kaalek was being ridiculous. Not to mention sexist and insulting.

Who did he think he was, telling me I couldn't help with the plan to sabotage the imperial forces on Carlogia? I was the one who made friends with Fenrey first. If I'd had to rely on the Raas' charms, we'd still be huddling outside. Or shot by imperial soldiers.

And he knew I wasn't some weak woman who fainted at the sight of blood, or ran when faced with danger. I'd stood up to him, hadn't I? Multiple times.

"I should have killed him when I had the chance," I said under my breath, the tunnel echoing my words back to me.

Not that I'd ever come close to being able to kill the huge warrior. He was fast and strong and battle-tested—all things that made me want to strive to keep up with him. I'd always pushed myself and found others to help me level up. I believed in doing things *before* you were ready for them and never backing down from a challenge. I hadn't known anything about captaining a ship before I won my freighter, but I'd learned on the job and taken advice from other commanders I'd met at outposts and fueling stations. The fact that Kaalek refused to let me be in the thick of the battle with him was frustrating beyond belief.

I heaved in a breath and leaned against the wall, slapping one open palm against the dirt. I hated feeling powerless. It was something I'd been running from my entire life. The fear of not being in control of my destiny was something I despised, and I'd done just about anything I could to avoid it. I'd take risk over that any day. Sure, I'd had to do a lot of things I hadn't liked, but they had been my choice, and they'd all gotten me one step closer to my goal of being free and able to take care of myself and my sister.

I squeezed my eyes shut. Of course, Astrid was gone now, so I didn't have her to take care of, and I was separated from my crew. If I couldn't take care of them, then at least I could help the Carlogians. But now, Kaalek wouldn't even let me do that.

I opened my eyes and smacked the wall again, grateful for the sharp sting. It was bad enough I'd ended up stranded with the jerk. Now he was making me feel like a useless woman, which I despised, because I was anything *but* that.

As I fumed in the tunnel, a loud thud made me jump. I glanced up to see that Kaalek had joined me underground.

"You!"

A muscle twitched in his jaw when he spotted me. "I do not wish to argue with you anymore, Tara."

"You don't want to fight with me? Then let me help."

He pushed past me. "You will help most by staying here and assisting Fenrey."

"Assisting Fenrey?" My voice rose to a near shriek as I followed him. "He doesn't need me here. You're the one who needs backup, and I'm the best one to go with you. I'm the only one who can go with you."

He stopped, spinning and glowering at me. "And I said that I don't want you."

His words should have hurt, but I was too furious to let them strike deep. "If you'd cut out the Vandar Raas bullshit, you could admit that you need me. Everyone else can see that I'm smart and capable. Why can't you?"

"This has nothing to do with your abilities, although I think you have never been in a true battle. Just because you have the heart of a warrior does not mean you fight like one."

"That's the stupidest—" I started to yell, then paused. "Did you just say that I have the heart of a warrior?"

"You did attempt to kill a Raas of the Vandar on his ship, in his own quarters, with a decorative battle axe you ripped from the wall. Your actions might have been foolish and pointless, but they were brave."

"Why is this sounding less and less like a compliment?"

His face remained unyielding. "You might have the instincts of a fighter, Tara, but that does not mean that your lack of skills would not make you a liability."

The words were a punch to my midriff. "You think I would be a liability to you?"

"I know you would." He backed away from me. "And as a Raas, it is my job to know when a warrior is a weak link."

I had a hard time drawing a breath. No one had ever called me a weak link. I'd always been tougher and smarter. So tough that nothing I'd had to do ever affected me. At least, not for long. My ears rang as tears stung the backs of my eyes at the insult. I blinked hard. I never cried, and was not about to start now. Not in front of the asshole who thought I was weak.

Kaalek looked away from me but his jaw was tight.

"Bullshit," I said, after I'd had a moment to recover and to study his body language. "This isn't about me. This is about you and your pathetic need to be the big, strong Raas."

Something flared hot and dangerous in his eyes. He closed the distance between us in a single step, his body pinning me against the wall. "This is not about me being Raas, but you are right about one thing, it is about me." He wrapped a hand around my waist and jerked me so that I was flush against him, his tail wrapping around my legs. "I will not be the reason you get hurt. In a battle, I will not be able to ensure your safety, and I could not live with myself if you were injured—or worse."

"Wh-what?" I stammered as I tipped my head back to meet his molten gaze.

"As infuriating as you are and as much as I have fought against it, you fill my thoughts. And that makes me weak. A Raas cannot be weak."

"I thought you wanted to put me out an airlock."

"That is true." He tilted his head slightly. "But since there is no airlock on the planet, I will have to go with my backup plan."

I swallowed hard. "What's your backup plan?"

"Fuck you until you cannot walk."

When he crushed his mouth to mine, all rational thought left me. Surges of pleasure coursed through my body as his tongue parted my lips and ignited a slow burn between my legs. Arousal nearly made my knees buckle, but the wall and his hard body kept me upright.

I fought for breath as his mouth plundered mine, and when he ground his rigid length into me, I moaned.

I should not want this. I should not want him.

He was the raider warlord who'd taken me off my ship and had me tied to his bed. But he was also the one who'd carried me through the forest when I was hurt. My hands, which had been splayed on his chest, fisted the fabric of his tunic, pulling him into me even more.

Just like I was strangely compelled to argue with him, I *needed* to feel him. Even as his touch scorched my skin, I needed more of him. I lifted my hands and dragged them through his hair, pulling his face away from me and panting for breath. "I still think you're an arrogant asshole."

His eyes were nearly black with desire. He dragged the rough pad of his thumb across my bottom lip. "And I still think you're an impossible and stubborn female."

"Good," I said. "As long as we're clear."

With a contented growl, he set his mouth on me again, his hands moving deftly from my waist to cup my breasts. Through my vest, he rolled my nipples between his fingers and thumbs, and I arched my back in response.

I dropped my hands to his chest, fumbling with the hooks closing his tunic in the front, finally pulling it open and smoothing my palms across the hard planes of his chest. Without breaking his lock on my lips, he slid his hands down around my ass and lifted me so that my legs wrapped around his waist.

When he started walking, I tore my mouth from him. "What—?"

"I prefer not to fuck you in the tunnel," he said, "At least not the first time." Taking long strides into the secret bedroom, he dropped me back onto the bed. The lamp already flickered warm on the nightstand. He planted his arms on either side of me. "That is what you want, isn't it, Tara?"

My heart pounded, sending fire racing through my body. I gazed up at him, the black tunic hanging open to reveal his chiseled chest and the dark marks curling across it. At that moment, my desire for him was more than want.

"I don't want you, Kaalek. I need you."

"Need me to do what?" His voice teased as he leaned over me.

My body nearly vibrated with desire. "I need you to fuck me."

CHAPTER TWENTY-THREE

Kaalek

Tara begging me to fuck her made it almost impossible for me to go slow, not that I wanted to. I'd been denying myself the pleasure of her for too long and fighting my own urges since I first laid eyes on her. I tugged her pants off as she hastily unbuttoned her top, revealing the sheer black undergarments she'd had on when I'd first seen her.

"These have been in my way for too long," I said, yanking off the slip of fabric covering her sex and tossing it to the floor.

Her pupils flared, making her green eyes dark, and she let her legs fall open. As I gazed down at the pink flush of her folds and saw that they were already slick for me, I felt like a starved predator. With a guttural sound, I dropped to my knees, pulling her so that her legs were over my shoulders, and she was open to me.

"Kaalek," she murmured, wiggling her hips wantonly to get her sweet little cunt closer to my mouth.

My cock ached at the sight of her and how freely she was giving herself to me. I had never been one for shy females. I liked females who liked to be fucked and who knew how to take pleasure as well as give it. Nothing made me harder than a female's breathy moans as I made her come.

There was only a tiny strip of flamed-colored hair at the top of her sex, which I kissed before dragging my tongue down the length of her. She was soaked already, and the taste of her made my cock strain against my snug pants. I lapped at her, finding a slick little bud that made her suck in a sharp breath and dig her hands into my hair.

I glanced up and saw her eyes half-lidded with desire. "You like when I lick that?"

She nodded, bowing her back. "That's my clit."

Although I'd had females of many different species before, I'd never fucked a human female. This little bundle intrigued me, as did the way she jerked and moaned when I flicked my tongue over it. "I have never seen one of these clits before, but I like it."

I returned my mouth to her clit, and she let out a small keening noise as I sucked it, loving the sensation of it plumping up beneath my tongue. As I continued to suck and flick it, I slid one finger inside her, and she moaned even louder. Swiveling my finger, I moved it rhythmically in and out while working her clit.

Her noises became louder, and her hips jerked. I slid my finger out of her without stopping the movements of my tongue, dragging the tip of my tail between her folds as her body quivered. Her juices made the dark fur of my tail damp and easier to slide inside her.

Tara reared up, her eyes going to my face buried between her legs and my tail moving deeper into her tight heat. "Are you fucking me with your tail?" she gasped.

I raised my head and pushed my tail in deeper, the sensitive tip savoring her tightness. "Do you like it?"

She bit the corner of her bottom lip as she nodded, her eyes tracking my tail as it went in and out of her. "The fur feels so good."

I put my lips back on her clit sucking it hard as my tail stroked faster. After a few seconds, Tara screamed out my name and her body detonated, clenching the tip of my tail over and over as she spasmed around me.

I stood up and yanked my own pants down, my cock springing up to jut out from my body. Dragging my tail out of her, I notched my thick crown at her entrance. I met her eyes as I pushed into her, her warmth already stretching for me. Even though it had felt good to have my tail inside her, this was even better.

I forced myself to swallow a cry as I held just the crown of my cock inside her. She was so tight and so wet for me. I wanted to go slow, but I couldn't. Not when the blood was pounding in my ears, and Tara was writhing beneath me, letting out breathy moans.

"You don't have to stop," she said between ragged breaths. "I promise I can take all of you."

That did nothing to help my self-control. I bent over her, crushing my mouth to hers. I had to taste her and her sweet tongue again.

Tara kissed me back hard, her tongue thrashing with mine and her fingers scraping through my hair, tugging my head closer to hers. As she kissed me with desperate wanting, my hips jerked forward. I plunged deep, lodging my cock all the way inside her with a single hard thrust. Then I held myself deep, savoring the delicious tightness of her.

Wrapping her arms around my back, she dug her nails into my flesh. "More," she commanded, tearing her mouth from mine. "I want you to fuck me hard, Kaalek."

She was so small compared to me, but she'd taken all of me and was begging for more. I knew I should go slow, but I couldn't. Not when she was begging for it, and not after I'd imagined how she'd feel around my cock too many times. Her tight little cunt was magic, and her breathy cries made it impossible for me not to respond.

"You are sure?" I said between gritted teeth as I dragged myself out, missing the tightness of her instantly.

"You're a Raas, right?" She teased. "Then show me how a big, tough raider claims a female. Or I'll have to find a Vandar who will."

The thought of another male burying his cock inside her made me pound myself back inside with a possessive roar. "No one else can have you."

"Then you'd better fuck me so hard I won't ever want any other Vandar again."

I slid my hands to her hips, my fingers biting into her flesh as I thrust myself again. My body hummed with a million sensations at once as I stroked my cock into her tight heat, feeling every tremor as she ran her hands down my back, her touch branding me.

I drove in again and again, unable to slow my savage rhythm as her gasps became screams. Rearing up, I scooped my hands under her ass without pausing, lifting her hips and hooking her legs over my shoulders.

Her breathing became faster and her cries more desperate. I wouldn't have been surprised if the sounds echoed down the tunnels and up into every house and shop along the way. I didn't care. The only thing that mattered was experiencing every moment of Tara's pleasure.

Holding myself inside her, I stared down at where our bodies met. The look of her pale skin being split by my cock—and seeing the dark swirls on my shaft disappear into her again and again—made a possessive growl escape my throat.

"You like to watch me stretched around your cock?" she asked, and I looked up to see her eyes flashing at me.

Heat flared in my core, but I couldn't speak. I lifted her hips higher and plunged deeper, curling my tail around to brush against her nub with each hard stroke.

Her eyelids fluttered and her fingers gripped my shoulders as I braced myself over her with both hands. She arched back, her teeth biting at her lower lip and her fingers digging fiercely into my skin.

The pain barely registered as her body begin to ripple, and her husky moans became cries. I thrust harder as her muscles clamped around my cock so tightly I had to squeeze my eyes shut. Black spots danced behind my eyelids as I lost all control, my release a furious rush of heat as I threw my head back and roared, emptying into her.

Tara gripped my slick shoulders, trembling and panting. My heart thundered in my chest as I slipped her legs back down and rested my forehead on hers, our shallow breaths mingling until I didn't know which were mine and which were hers.

CHAPTER TWENTY-FOUR

Tara

I heaved in a jerky breath, letting my legs slide down. "That was..."

"Mm-hmm." His head was touching mine as our heavy panting gave way to regular breathing.

I put a palm flat on his slick chest, and the thudding belied his heart's rapid beat. At least my body wasn't the only one still coming down from the high. His curling marks peeked through my splayed fingertips, and I traced one swirl with the tip of my finger. "I like these, but I've always liked tattoos on guys."

"They aren't tattoos." He lifted me, and then dropped us both down so that we were fully on the bed. He rolled onto his back and pulled me with him so that I was half on him and half on the bed.

"Right. You're born with them."

He nodded, absently running one hand down my bare hip as he held me to him.

I waited for him to say more, but he was silent. "Are they all the same?"

His chest rose and fell. "No. Each Vandar male has marks that are unique to him, and then they change when he takes his true mate."

He'd mentioned this before when telling me about my sister and his brother, but it was still hard to believe. I'd always found the concept of true mates to be odd and a bit stifling. I didn't want biology dictating who I should be with, or that I should be with anyone at all. The more males I'd encountered throughout the galaxy, the more I'd valued my independence. "Humans don't have anything like that."

"I know." He didn't meet my eyes.

I continued tracing my finger around his marks. "When your mating marks appear on a female, you become a matching set?"

"I suppose, although I would not phrase it like that." He cut his eyes to me. "If his mate is true, the male's marks also extend farther down his chest and arms. I saw that on my brother."

My hand stilled. "You mean Kratos, the Raas who has my sister?"

"The Raas who is mated to your sister," he corrected. "The marks could not have appeared if she was being held against her will."

I pressed my lips together. It was hard to wrap my head around the idea of timid Astrid willingly becoming the mate of a Vandar warlord. Then again, I never could have imagined that I would have found myself in bed with one. As much as I'd fought it, I couldn't bring myself to regret it. He might make me crazy, but he also drove me wild, and I wasn't above having a little fun. Or a lot.

I finally huffed out a breath. "Okay, I guess I'll believe you, although I'd like to talk to her and make sure she's okay."

Laughter shook his body. "You make a lot of demands for someone who is not in charge."

"You think you're in charge?" I let my hand wander from his chest down his corded stomach until I grasped his cock. It had not softened, and my touch made it instantly become more rigid. "Why don't you tell me about the marks on this?"

"You want to talk about the marks on my cock?" His voice was hesitant as I wiggled my body down the length of his.

When my mouth reached his cock, I glanced up at him, my hand wrapped snugly around the base of his shaft. "Why not? These don't transfer onto your true mate, do they?"

He choked out a laugh. "No." As I traced my tongue around one swirling dark mark, he clenched his jaw. "But that is not why you are doing this."

I licked the tip of his crown, and his body jerked beneath me. "So cynical."

"Tara." His voice was sharp, even though his hands fisted the bed covers.

"Fine," I said. "I thought maybe you'd reconsider taking me with you to the mine."

"This is how you will convince me?" He asked, biting down hard on his bottom lip.

I swirled my tongue around his crown and grinned up at him. "Is it working?"

"A little."

I stopped licking. "So, you'll let me come with you?"

He groaned. "You really think this will work?"

"I don't know." I teased the tip of his cock with my tongue. "Do you want me to suck your cock or not?"

"Who is ruthless now?" He expelled a loud breath. "You can come."

I took his entire crown in my mouth and sucked, looking up and seeing him watching me, his gaze molten. I released him and smiled. "Was that so hard?"

Pushing myself up so that I was on all fours between his legs, I took him in my mouth again, moving up and down his thick length. Something that I'd never really relished before was suddenly a huge turn-on—emphasis on the huge— especially when he moaned and tangled his hands in my hair to guide me.

Knowing how hard I was making him and hearing his appreciative noises made my body heat in response and my nipples pebble. So, when the furry tip of his tail moved between my legs again, I didn't hesitate to spread them for him.

"Two can play," he said, as his tail stroked through my folds, which were still wet, finding my clit and swirling around it.

I moaned, the vibrations from my mouth buzzing against his cock and making him growl. I took him as far as I could, squeezing my throat and dragging my mouth slowly down his length. He gripped my hair, but his tail never stopped moving, and soon I was trembling with a fast release, my body jerking but my cries muffled by the cock in my mouth.

I pulled back for a moment, wiping the side of my mouth. "You have an unfair advantage with your tail."

"You wish me to stop using it?" He asked, moving it down and teasing it at my opening.

I shook my head, taking him in my mouth again and sucking as he slid his tail inside me. I was still quivering from my release, and my body clenched around the tip of his tail rhythmically.

"Gods of old, your cunt is so tight," he gritted out. "I can't hold back any longer."

"Don't," I told him, my voice breathy. "I want to swallow every last drop of you."

That seemed to push him over the edge. As I took him deep in my throat, he clenched his hands in my hair and held me to him as he pulsed hot and fast into me. I swallowed, almost distracted by the steady thrusts of his tail and the tingling feeling that was building in my core again.

I tore my mouth away from him, and he sagged back against

the bed. But he was hardly resting. His tail was working me so well I was arching my ass up and moaning.

"You like my tail inside you?"

My eyes were closed, and I'd bent down so that my lips were brushing his stomach. I couldn't speak but I managed to nod. This Vandar had done what no one else ever had. He'd rendered me speechless. I clenched the sheets as I started to come again, although I felt like I'd really never stopped. I bucked up, gripping his tail tight as Kaalek buried it deep inside me, then screaming as light exploded across my eyelids.

When I finally collapsed on top of him, he dragged his tail out of me. He pulled me up and tucked me so that I could rest one cheek on his chest muscle.

"You don't play fair," I said once I'd caught my breath.

He laughed, the gravelly sound echoing in my chest. "You didn't enjoy that?"

I swatted at his chest. "You know I did."

"What is the problem?"

Actually, I wasn't sure. I couldn't exactly complain about being fucked *too* well, although I was pretty sure my power play had gotten turned around on me. Not that I really cared. It wasn't like I was still the Vandar's captive, or that he'd even treated me like one since we'd crashed on the planet.

"So, what is this?" I finally asked.

"What is what?"

I sighed. The alien was still infuriating. "You and me. I'm clearly not your prisoner anymore."

"Why do you say that?" He held me closer. "I think you are mine now more than ever."

"Just because of *that*?"

"You mean because I claimed you with my cock and my tail? Do not tell me that other males have made you moan like that."

He was right. They hadn't. "That doesn't mean you own me."

He rolled me over on my back and pinned me down. His

face hovered above mine, his gaze scorching. "You are mine, Tara. Your breathy sighs and wild hair and your tight heat. You can try to deny it, but that would be a lie."

My heart stuttered. "I'm the captain of my own ship."

"Not anymore."

"Do you really think I'd give up my life just to...what...be your permanent booty call?"

His eyes held mine. "I could imagine worse things." Then he crushed his mouth to mine and there was no more talking.

CHAPTER TWENTY-FIVE

Kaalek

I pulled on my clothes in the dark, grateful I couldn't see her sleeping while I dressed. Even if her eyes had been closed, the sight of her untamed curls spilling across the pillow would have made it harder for me to leave. I tugged on the pants with a sharp jerk, angry at my weakness. I had left many females behind before. Why was it so hard to walk away from this one?

It shouldn't matter that she was different from all the pleasures I'd been with, or that she was the only female who'd ever challenged me. She was still a female, and one I'd taken captive. I could not allow myself the indulgence of caring for her. As much as I'd loved being inside her, she was a weakness a Raas could not afford.

What about your promise? The voice in the back of my head whispered. *A Raas does not lie.*

But a Raas did not also let his mate go into danger. I paused. She was not my mate. And as right as it felt when she was with me—and when I was inside her—I knew she would never be mine. What happened to Kratos was an aberration. Females who were not Vandar could not get mating marks. Not that Tara had any desire to be my mate. As much as she loved me inside her and took pleasure in arguing with me, she still wished to leave me and return to her ship. She was not an untouched, unexperienced female who would expect passion to equal anything more, which was one of the reasons she appealed so much and why I needed to put distance between us.

When I'd hooked my tunic in the front, I reached for my battle axe, the cold steel familiar beneath my fingers. The curved blade calmed me, even though it had run red with blood more times than I could count.

It was better this way. She would be angry, but she would be safe. That was most important.

I inhaled the loamy scent of the dirt surrounding me and took careful steps out of the hidden room and down the tunnel away from the tailor's shop. I did not want to disturb him, but most of all, I did not want him to know I'd left. I liked the Carlogian, but I thought he might feel more loyalty to Tara or might agree that she should be allowed to go with me. The less the little alien knew, the better.

Fenrey had told me how far the tunnel extended and where it came out at the far end, so I moved quickly on soft feet, one hand outstretched to the side so I would not run into the curved walls. The string lights weren't illuminated so blackness engulfed me, and the only indication that I was still in the tunnel was the occasional ladder my fingers brushed against as I passed an entrance to one of the overhead buildings. I didn't know who I was running underneath, but I imagined the Carlogians sleeping soundly in small, cozy dwellings above me.

When the tunnel began to slope up, I slowed my pace. Fenrey had told me that the entrance into the woods and near the dirt road leading to the mines would be after the tunnel angled up. After another few strides, I was bumping my hands across the wooden rungs of a ladder.

I pulled myself up hand over hand until I reached a trapdoor. Pushing it open, I found myself in the middle of a wooded area, light from two tiny moons creating shadowy outlines of trees. I closed the trapdoor behind me, noticing that greenery had been fastened to the top, so it looked like a small bush. It blended in so perfectly with the surroundings, I doubted I would be able to find it again.

"If we are victorious, then I will not need to hide in a tunnel," I said to myself. "If we are not, I will probably not be returning to the village."

The thought weighed heavily on me, and my heart clenched as I thought about Tara. I shook my head. This was why I could not think about her. She was a distraction, as was any thought of her soft skin or her legs spread open for me. My cock twitched to life, and I let out an exasperated huff.

Focus, Kaalek. You need to think about killing imperial soldiers, not fucking the human.

I pressed my cock down as it strained against my pants, ignoring the uncomfortable throb as I scanned the woods for a path. If I was not careful, I'd be caught by imperial sentries because I was so distracted by my aching cock. Another reason I should not have given in to my body's aching desires. But what was done was done. Now I needed to focus on the mission—killing imperial soldiers.

I stayed motionless, letting my cock soften and my eyes adjust to the night. Darkness was what Vandar preferred anyway, so the dim lighting was welcome. My ears pricked at the sound of movement, but I quickly assessed that it was a small animal moving through the undergrowth, and not a Zagrath soldier. Aside from the crunching of branches, the only noises were the songs of night insects. After living on a ship for so long, natural noises were foreign to my ears, although I quickly became accustomed to their rhythm.

After I ascertained that there were no Zagrath nearby, I moved stealthily toward a break in the undergrowth. When I reached it, I saw that it led to a path which fed into a dirt road wide enough for a procession of soldiers. As I stepped onto the hard-packed dirt, I could almost imagine the conscripted Carlogians being marched to the mines with imperial soldiers flanking them.

I'd already seen how clever and skilled the natives were. Forcing them to mine deep in the earth displayed, once again, the empire's cruel disregard for other cultures in its pursuit of wealth and power. Just as they had done with my people.

I tightened my grip on my battle axe. Soon, there would be no more Carlogians forced to work in mines by the empire.

"For Vandar." The familiar battle cry, although whispered, made my pulse quicken in anticipation. Glancing behind me and seeing nothing, I took off running in the direction Fenrey had told me.

It had been a while since I'd run, but I welcomed the stretch of my legs and the warming of my lungs. Even the air was not as humid as I'd remembered it, and I drew in deep breaths. Every so often, I paused to listen and watch, but I was not being followed. Zagrath soldiers—with their helmets and laser rifles—did not move quietly, so if they were behind me, I would have heard them.

The element of surprise was crucial for my mission, especially since I had no backup. It was unusual for a Vandar warrior to go into any battle by himself. It was why we flew in hordes and attacked in an amoeba formation. There was strength in numbers and power in overwhelming your opponents. If I was lucky, my horde had picked up my beacon and was on its way to Carlogia Prime now. If not, I would have to hope that the villagers' plan went off without a flaw. Even then, our success relied on my horde providing much-needed firepower.

"They'll come," I said under my breath. My *majak* and battle chief had fought by my side for long enough to know my mind. Even without a beacon to guide them, they would know what I would do, and where I would have gone. They would come to Carlogia Prime and secure the victory. "I'm counting on you, brothers."

I murmured a quick incantation to Lokken, the ancient god of the Vandar, even though it had been a long time since I'd prayed to our gods. "Let me be victorious, Lokken, god of old. And if it is my day to die, let me live on in Zedna, with the warriors who have gone before me." I blew out a hot breath, adding softly, "But let it not be today."

Fenrey had said that the mine was half a day's walk, but half a day of a Carlogian walking on short legs was a far cry from a Vandar Raas running at a fast pace. Soon, the road became harder, which meant that heavy objects had most likely moved over it. The mine was close.

I slowed my pace to a walk, clutching my axe across my chest. I still couldn't hear imperial soldiers, but they could always be hiding. I tipped my head back to look for sentry posts high in trees, but saw none.

If there was a mine nearby, where was the sound? I knew from past missions onto planets the Zagrath had mined, that they ran their operations continuously, working miners in shifts so there was never a time when production stopped. The empire was too greedy to allow for anything else. It was to their advantage to strip the planet as fast as they could before my people could get wind of it and ruin their plans.

It made me smile when I thought about how many Zagrath operations we'd crippled. It was no wonder the empire was so desperate to make us out to be the criminals. As long as the

Vandar hordes ruled the skies, they would never have full dominion over the galaxy.

"As it should be," I muttered to myself, my chest swelling with pride at the thought of the Vandar hordes ruling the heavens.

I spotted a flash of something through the forest ahead, but I could not tell what it was. Was it the aboveground structure of the mine, or the shine of an imperial helmet? I stopped and moved to the edge of the road, peering through the trees. Whatever it was, it wasn't moving. I eased one foot forward, careful not to make a sound.

"Not another step, hot stuff."

I whirled toward the voice, freezing when I found myself surrounded by a bizarre group of aliens, blasters and curved blades pointed at me. They were not Zagrath, but they did not look friendly, either.

Tvek.

CHAPTER TWENTY-SIX

Tara

"Greetings of the morn!" Fenrey's voice came just after the glow of light from the tunnel. I blinked a few times and pulled the covers higher around me, since I was naked underneath. My gaze went to the clothes strewn across the floor. No time to scoop them up before the Carlogian came into the room, so I'd just have to play it off.

I reached my foot out to nudge Kaalek, but my leg stretched all the way across the bed without touching him. I rolled over to find that he wasn't in bed, at all. My gaze went back to the floor. Only my clothes remained. His were gone, as was his battle axe that had been propped in the corner.

"He wouldn't have," I said to myself, a mixture of disbelief and irritation flaring inside me.

When Fenrey entered the room, he pointedly ignored the clothing on the floor, stepping over it and putting a tray with two mugs and two plates of Carlogian biscuits on the empty side of the bed. My heart sank as his brow furrowed, causing more wrinkles to crease his face than usual.

"So Kaalek isn't already upstairs?" I asked.

"No, dear." His gaze took in the small room, as if the huge Vandar warrior could have been hiding behind one of the side tables.

"That bastard went ahead without me." After everything that had happened and everything that had been said, he'd moved up the plan and left without me. I probably shouldn't have been surprised—he had been pretty adamant that I not be put in danger—but the betrayal stung.

I bit the inside of my mouth until I tasted blood. He wasn't the first guy who'd snuck out of my bed, but it was usually the other way around, and I usually didn't care so much.

That thought led to another one. Why did I care so much? He was still the raider warlord who'd thought it was fine to take me as his personal prisoner. He was bossy, possessive, and had some serious family issues. I should have been thrilled he was gone. But I wasn't.

Despite all his faults—and there were some serious ones—he was the first person I'd let get close to me in a long time. The first person I'd trusted. And he'd left me. Just like my parents and just like Astrid.

I swallowed the metallic tang of blood and realized that I'd balled the blanket in my fists.

Fenrey was staring at me. "I'm sure he'll be back, dear."

"I'm sure he won't," I muttered, then forced myself to meet Fenrey's eyes. "He's gone ahead to the mine. He's putting the plan into motion without me. It's the only reason he would have left in the dark."

"Oh." Fenrey's expression was sympathetic, then he jumped as if he'd been stung. "If that's the case, then we need to get things going on this end." He bustled from the room, pausing in the arched doorway and looking back. "Eat up and come upstairs as soon as you can. We still need you, dear."

"Thanks." I gave him a weak smile, then he hurried off down the tunnel toward the ladder leading to his shop.

He was right. The Carlogians *did* need me, even if Kaalek was too arrogant to realize that he did. I chugged my tea and then tossed back Kaalek's as well. After I gathered my clothes, I dressed and grabbed one of the biscuits, munching it as I walked down the tunnel and climbed up the ladder.

Even before I pushed through the curtain to the front of the shop, the excited chatter of voices reached my ears. Had I slept in again?

"There she is," Coxley said, when I emerged from behind the doorway curtain. "How's that ankle?"

"Like new," I told him.

He winked at me. "Just in time for today."

"I won't be running anywhere. Kaalek left without me."

The conversation halted, and everyone swung their heads to me.

"That's why I said we needed to pick up the pace," Fenrey said, waving for the villagers to join him at the worktable. He rolled out the map that Kaalek had marked yesterday. "If the Vandar is already on his way to the mine, we need to make sure the imperial soldiers here are taken care of. We don't want the mine calling for reinforcements."

"They can call all they want," Coxley said. "As long as there's no one to answer."

Fenrey clapped him on the back. "Well said, my friend."

"You don't need to worry about the explosions," Brylynn said, leaning both hands on his cane. "Rix and I worked through the night. The wires are laid, and the charges are active. Right, Rix?"

There was no answer, and I glanced around the room,

finding the Carlogian chemist sitting in a chair, with his head tipped back, and his eyes closed.

"Rix!" Brylynn's gruff voice boomed throughout the space, and Rix woke suddenly, jumping and slipping out of the chair and onto the floor with a thud.

"Ow!" He looked around, scowling. "Why'd you have to yell like that?"

The old Carlogian sighed. "I was telling everyone about our explosives."

Rix's frown became a grin as he stood up, rubbing his backside. "They're good to go, and we won't have to worry about any of our neighbors happening on them. Anyone who isn't part of the resistance is currently enjoying a very long slumber, thanks to some delicious pastries filled with cream and sleeping draught."

The village baker beamed and curtsied as everyone clapped. "I delivered them personally, and insisted they eat one on the spot and give me their opinion on my new hurly-flower cream."

"Hurley-flower." Fenrey rubbed his own belly. "That sounds tasty."

She twitched one shoulder. "It's the only thing sweet enough to mask the taste of the chemicals."

"No retching?" I asked.

"We thought this would be less suspicious and less messy," she said.

"What about the tunnels?" I scanned the room for the carpenter, but didn't see him. "Will they be able to withstand the explosions?"

"Taiko is working on the extra supports." Fenrey tapped the map. "He started at the village end of the tunnel and is working his way down. I checked on him when I came down to deliver your breakfast. He's probably finished by now. He cut the wood last night and then brought it in through the tunnels. He hasn't rested yet either."

Guilt stabbed at me. While the Carlogians had been working diligently, Kaalek and I had been fucking each other's brains out. Now that I thought about it, if they'd been using the tunnels to move around, they'd probably all heard us. My face burned with embarrassment and fresh anger at Kaalek for leaving me to be the only one to face the villagers the morning after. When I saw him again, I was going to kill him.

"There's only one thing left to do," Fenrey said, leaning back with his hands braced on the table. "We need to give the Zagrath soldiers a reason to run over our explosives."

"I thought about this." Coxley steepled his fingers as he spoke. "Most of them are either at the garrison post at the other end of the village, or will be staggering out of the public house. All we have to do is create a distraction at this end dramatic enough to bring them all running."

"I can take care of that," I said, before anyone else could volunteer.

Fenrey frowned. "I didn't think we wanted the empire to know you were here. We certainly don't want them to capture you."

"If they get blown up, they won't be able to capture me," I said. "Just keep the trapdoor to the tunnel open and ready. Then close it right behind me. I'll hide down there, in case any of them actually make it through the gauntlet."

Fenrey didn't look so sure, but the elder Carlogian slapped his hand on the table. "Let the girl do it. She can probably cause more of a ruckus showing her face than anything the rest of us could think up."

"A human female in the village would create a stir," Coxley admitted.

Fenrey held up his palms in submission. "Fine, but we'll be waiting for you with the trap door ready." He then turned and pulled a dark coat off a hook. "Here. I made this for you to wear."

The fabric was slightly iridescent, and thick. I pulled it on and smoothed my hands down the long sleeves. It fell to below my knees and buttoned in the front, and looked somewhat like the tunic he'd made for Kaalek. Like everything the tailor had made, it fit like a glove.

"Thanks, Fenrey."

He nodded, his brow creasing. "Promise me you'll keep it on?"

"Sure," I said, tilting my head at him.

He nodded. "Good. Your pale skin draws too much attention. This will help you blend in, and it will keep you warm."

"Warm?" The planet seemed steamy to me, but maybe my internal temperature was different than the locals.

"Carlogia Prime is tropical during the day, but the temperatures drop significantly at night," he said. "If you have not been outside when the sun falls, you might be surprised."

"Thanks, Fenrey." I grinned at him. It had been a long time since anyone had worried about me like a parent would, and my throat tightened as the Carlogian patted me on the arm. I winked at him, and then took a few steps toward the door.

"Now?" Coxley said, staring at both of us. "You're doing it now?"

I pivoted to see all the villagers gaping at me. "If Kaalek is already headed to the mines, we don't have time to waste." I didn't say that if the stubborn Vandar had waited for me, we wouldn't be in such a rush. At this point, it would be a miracle if his horde arrived to join the battle in time, but I didn't want to tell them that. Not when they'd worked so hard. No, I'd wait until I saw Kaalek, and then give him an extra kick in the balls on their behalf.

Fenrey pulled back the curtain over the doorway leading to the rear of his shop, and gave me a single nod. "Don't worry. We'll be ready."

I returned his sharp nod, stepping from the shop and

walking to the middle of the street. Falling to my knees, I let out the loudest scream I could. Then I screamed again, and finally some soldiers appeared at the far end of the village, but they didn't move toward me.

"Help," I cried. "I just escaped from a Vandar raider! He's right behind me!"

That did it. Soldiers appeared from several doorways and sprinted toward me. I didn't move until the first explosion sent two soldiers flying into the air. Then I jumped up and bolted back into Fenrey's shop. I dashed through the front room, which was now empty, and ran to the hatch that Fenrey held open. He patted me on the back as I hurried down the ladder, then the door slammed shut over my head. When I reached the bottom, I saw that all the Carlogians were gathered around the ladder as explosions shook the ground and dust sifted down from above.

"It worked," I said, my heart hammering in my chest. "Now, I've got one more thing to do."

I took off running down the tunnel. Kaalek was going to get backup whether he wanted it or not.

CHAPTER TWENTY-SEVEN

Kaalek

"Don't even think about making a move toward that axe." The voice was sharp and authoritative, but also female.

My gaze went to the female with dark curls piled on top of her head, and brown skin with bumps running above her brows. A Zevrian. I'd usually known the alien species to travel in groups as mercenaries, but the others with her were not Zevrians. I recognized one pale-haired one as human, but the rest were gold-skinned males with long, black hair and bare chests.

"Who are you?" I kept my eyes on the blaster aimed at my heart and stilled the fingers hovering over my weapon.

"We're the bounty hunters who're going to take you in," the Zevrian said.

"The bounty hunter babes," the human added.

The Zevrian winced. "I thought we agreed not to call ourselves that anymore since the Dothveks are with us."

The human shrugged. "I still like it." She focused her gaze on me. "We're the best in the galaxy, so don't even think about trying to get away."

The huge, gold creatures hadn't spoken yet, and I let my gaze move over them, assessing their stance and weapons. Instead of blasters, they held curved blades that glinted in the moonlight, but I had a feeling they were skilled with them. I'd never heard of Dothveks, but there were plenty of planets I'd never visited.

"The Zagrath sent you?" I asked, not moving a muscle.

The Zevrian shifted from one foot to the other. "It was a human captain who put out a bounty on your head, but we know the empire will pay handsomely for a Vandar raider."

"Especially one who abducted a human," the light-haired one said with a frown.

"A human issued the bounty?" I almost groaned out loud. "I don't think you have the right Vandar."

The Zevrian's brow furrowed as the human shot a look at her.

"I am not Raas Kratos. My brother is the one who took the human female from a freighter and was pursued across the sector because of it. The captain who put a bounty out on his head was probably the female's sister." I had an urge to laugh. Of course, Tara had issued a bounty, even though she most likely couldn't pay for it. She was bold and impulsive, and it was exactly what I would have done, if I'd been in her shoes.

The gold-skinned males exchanged glances, but didn't speak.

"Tor—" the human started, but the Zevrian cut her off.

She narrowed her dark eyes. "I don't believe you. We got reports that a Vandar and human crashed on this planet."

"Reports?" I asked.

"The empire knows you're here," the Zevrian gave me a menacing smile, her pointed teeth flashing. "And we're good at intercepting imperial transmissions."

I eyed the group. They were armed and informed, and I

wasn't going to be able to fight my way through them. My next best option was the truth. "The empire is right. I am here with a human. But I'm not Raas Kratos. And the human is not the one who was taken from the freighter. It's the captain who issued the bounty."

The Zevrian tilted her head at me. "Please don't insult my intelligence by telling me that you're assisting the human captain in finding her sister. I know enough about the Vandar to know that you aren't bounty hunters."

"You're correct. We do not hunt bounties. We fight against the empire for the freedom of the galaxy."

The human's blaster dropped slightly. "Is that what you're doing on Carlogia Prime?"

"Actually, yes." I squared my shoulders. "I am Raas Kaalek of the Vandar. My horde was en route to this planet to liberate them from the empire when we were tracked and attacked. The human and I were separated from the horde and crashed here. My warbirds should be here at any time to join the fight."

"Fight?" The alien with dark slashes across his chest muscles spoke, his voice a deep rumble. "We have seen no fight."

"Insurrections are not always so obvious at first," I told him. "The human and I have been working with the local resistance in a nearby village. While they create a distraction, my task is to liberate the natives working in the mines." I decided to omit the fact that I'd jump-started the plan by running out on Tara.

"Mines?" Another gold-skinned alien asked, this one with dark bands ringing his thick arms.

I resisted the urge to let out an impatient sigh. "The empire has determined that this pre-warp planet contains rare minerals, which they need to power their technology. They have conscripted the natives to mine for the minerals, and posted soldiers to prevent the natives from protesting or rising up."

"Did you know about this, Danica?" one of the gold-skinned males asked the humans.

She shook her head, frowning. "How do we know this is true?"

"You aren't seriously thinking of believing this Vandar, are you?" The Zevrian gaped at her. "For all we know, he kidnapped the human captain and is holding her against her will, and this story about the Carlogian resistance is just that—a story to elicit our sympathy and let him go."

A low growl escaped my lips. "A Raas of the Vandar does not lie."

"Which is what you'd say if you were lying about all this," the Zevrian said.

I could sense the hesitation among the group. They were not sure what to believe. Just then, a rumble shook the ground beneath our feet.

My gaze went behind me to where I knew the village was. *Tvek.* They'd started. I should have been at the mine already, waiting to spring into action and liberate the natives before the Zagrath could realize it was a set-up and a trap to lure them away. But instead, I was stuck talking to a bunch of bounty hunters who could very well decide to take me to their ship and throw me in the brig.

Another rumble—this one louder—and then smoke rose up in the distance, silhouetted again the night sky, which was fading to blue. I bit back in impatient growl. "That's the Carlogian resistance providing a distraction. I suggest we hide before the Zagrath soldiers run over us on their way to offer assistance to their fellow soldiers."

The Zevrian stared at me and then squinted at the faint outline of smoke. Behind us in the other direction, engines revved, and voices rose.

"Come on, Tori." The human tugged at the Zevrian's arm. "I think he might be right. It sounds like someone is headed for the explosions."

The Zevrian who was clearly called Tori gave a curt nod,

then waved at me with her blaster. "Okay, I'm giving you the benefit of the doubt, Vandar. But only because I don't particularly like imperial soldiers. This doesn't mean I buy your entire story, and if you try to run or attack us, I will blow your head off."

"Understood." I followed her waving blaster as we moved behind a thick copse of bushes.

Crouching down, we watched as imperial soldiers in dark helmets zoomed by on sleek hoverpods. I counted at least ten, clenching my jaw and hoping the villagers were well hidden and that Tara was safe. Part of me wanted to race back to the village and help them with the incursion of soldiers, but I knew that was not my mission. I *had* to get to the mine, or the villagers work would be for nothing.

When the soldiers had passed, the human straightened. "Okay, Raas Kaalek. You were right about the soldiers."

"I told you, a Raas does not lie." I inclined my head in the direction the soldiers had come from. "If the Carlogian resistance is right, the mine should be up ahead, and hopefully now it will be less fortified. I need to go now so I can get the natives out before the soldiers return."

"You were on your way there when we stopped you?" the alien with the dark slashes across his chest asked.

"Yes. My mission is to liberate the Carlogians who have been forced to work in the mines. That way, they will not be injured when my horde arrives and destroys it."

The Zevrian blinked at me rapidly. "Your plan is to blow up the mine?"

I did not have time to explain, but I talked fast. "Once my horde arrives, I will give the order to destroy it. The Carlogians do not need the rare minerals. Only the empire wants them. If I destroy the mine, I make the planet less appealing for them."

"Won't the empire just rebuild it?" the human asked, stepping closer to the alien with the dark chest markings.

"Then we will destroy it again," I said. "Until they leave Carlogia Prime in peace."

The human gave me a small grin. "You're even more stubborn than Tori."

Tori cut her eyes to the female, affection obvious in her gaze even as she pursed her lips. "Then we'd better haul ass. I, for one, don't want to be in the mine when it blows."

I stared at her for a moment. "What?"

Tori shook her head. "You don't think we're going to let you have all the fun, do you?"

"You believe me?"

She cocked her head at me. "Our pilot is no fan of the empire, and she used to fly for a rebel group. She said something about the Vandar not being what the empire makes them out to be."

"I thought you tuned Caro out," the human said.

"Trust me," Tori said. "Sometimes I do, but some of the things she natters on about get through. I guess this was one of them." She swung on me, her blaster still high. "I might believe you about the empire, but you still haven't explained why you're here with a human. If I find out you're holding her somewhere against her will, don't think I won't shoot you."

"You have my word she's not being held captive," I said. I thought about how hard it had been to leave her in the warm bed where our bodies had been tangled together. My heart squeezed. No, it was not her who was the captive.

Tori grunted and jerked her head in the direction of the mine. As we all took off running, I only hoped Tara had been smart and stayed in the village.

CHAPTER TWENTY-EIGHT

Tara

I am so going to kill Kaalek when I find him, I thought, as I ran through the forest.

I had to keep my head down so I could follow the faint path in the undergrowth, although the diffused moonlight helped. It shone through the haze in the sky, making the moons like tiny, fuzzy glowing orbs. Sucking in a breath, I could smell the loamy soil and the moisture in the air. After spending so long in a climate-controlled spaceship, I enjoyed the unusual smells of the planet.

Fenrey had been right about the temperature. It was startling how much colder it was during the night than in the day. I was grateful for the coat he'd made me, and I rubbed a hand over one of the sleeves as I ran. My feet crunched the leaves and branches, but I couldn't bother trying to be quiet. I was already running to catch up.

A rumble shook the ground, and I paused and looked over

my shoulder. Most of the explosions had gone off before I'd made it down the length of the tunnel, dirt falling on me as I'd run and the beams shoring up the tunnel groaning from the pressure. My pulse had raced at the thought of the tunnel collapsing with me inside it, but I'd just run faster, and the beams had held it up.

Now, I looked at the puff of smoke behind me and hoped that the villagers were still safe. Most of them had been hiding in the tunnel, but Fenrey had stayed above to let me in through the trap door and close it behind me, hiding it with the rug.

"He'll be okay," I muttered to myself, as I turned back around and resumed running. The old Carlogian had proven himself to be clever and resourceful. If anyone could outsmart the Zagrath, it was him. I exhaled, seeing my own breath hover in the cold air, and picked up my pace. The best thing I could do for Fenrey now was find his son and bring him back.

The throaty hum of engines made me dive for cover, and a group of hoverpods flying in a V formation whizzed by me. Luckily I'd gotten out of the way in time. They hadn't spotted me or flattened me.

Standing, I glanced around and listened for more. Nothing. My stomach clenched when I realized that the hoverpods were heading for the village. The empire had sent reinforcements from the mine.

"That's good," I whispered. "It will be easier to take over the mine."

But I knew that meant the village would be overrun with Zagrath soldiers, looking for answers. I hoped they wouldn't find any.

I took off with renewed purpose, knowing that Kaalek must be near the mine by now. As much of a badass Vandar as he was, the chances of him pulling off the mission by himself were slim. But he couldn't fail. *We* couldn't fail.

Not that there was a *we*. He'd made that perfectly clear when he'd fucked me and then run away as fast as he could. I gritted my teeth, telling myself that I didn't need him, and I certainly didn't care about him.

The path grew into a wider dirt road and my steps became easier. After a little longer, I could see an opening in the trees and a flash of something shiny and metallic. *The mine.* I was almost there. I sucked in a breath—ignoring the ache in my side —and powered forward.

Something caught in my periphery moments before I was knocked off my feet. Instead of hitting the ground, I was suddenly hanging upside down.

"What did you just do?" A female voice asked.

"Tell me that isn't the human you crashed here with." This voice—also female—was less curious and more hostile.

Lifting my head, I saw several aliens surrounding me. I also saw that I was hanging down someone's back. Another moment and I knew whose back it was. Kaalek.

"You have two seconds to put me down before I break your legs," I said, pounding on him.

"I already like her," one of the females said.

Kaalek swung me down to the ground, holding me by the shoulders to steady me.

I swatted him away and glared at him. "Why the fuck did you tackle me?"

He glared back. "You were about to run straight at the mine and ruin our plan."

"Your plan? What about *our* plan?" I allowed myself to take in the group he was with now that they weren't upside down. There was a blonde and a female—not human—with dark curls, as well as two hulking, gold-skinned aliens wearing only pants. They were all staring at me as I fumed. I steadied my breath. "You mind introducing me to your friends? I know they're not Vandar or Carlogians."

"Right on both counts," the blonde said. "I'm Danica, leader

—well, one of them—of a bounty hunter crew." She jerked a thumb at the other woman. "This is Tori."

"Bounty hunters?" I peered at her. This pretty woman was a bounty hunter? Every bounty hunter I'd ever seen looked more like the guys she was with—or scarier.

"Yep." The dark-haired female spun a pointy metal stick in her hand. "From what your friend tells us, you're probably the reason we're here."

"Why would I be the rea...?" I almost smacked my own head. When Astrid had been taken from my ship, I had set a bounty for her rescue. I hadn't thought anything would come of it, since I'd also contacted the empire and they'd jumped at the chance to track down a Vandar horde. "You saw the transmission about the bounty on Raas Kratos?"

"Let me guess." The female she'd called Tori cut her eyes to Kaalek. "Your friend here isn't him."

I unclenched my fists. "First of all, we're not friends." I jerked my head toward Kaalek and noticed the gold-skinned males cock their slashed eyebrows. "But, I am the one who put a bounty out for the safe return of my sister. And Kaalek isn't the one who took her."

Danica let out a breath. "So, we went after the wrong human who was with a Vandar horde?"

I let my gaze slide to Kaalek. He still looked furious, but now he looked wary. I could tell them that he'd abducted me and that the Zagrath would reward them handsomely for his head, and he knew it. They were also better armed than he was, which was something I guessed he was also aware of.

As livid as I was at the arrogant Vandar, I decided against turning him in. I wanted to be the one to kick his ass. Not the empire or even these bounty hunters.

"Sorry," I said, looking back at the blonde. "He's right. It was me. But the bounty is a moot point now. I can't pay it, and apparently, my sister doesn't want to be rescued."

"Typical," the dark-haired female growled.

The blonde nudged her. "It's not a total loss, Tori. We still get to help liberate a planet from the empire."

The alien she'd called Tori gave her a grin. "It's not as good as credits, but it's something. These Zagrath do sound like a bunch of assholes, and we haven't had a good fight in a while."

The alien with dark bands around his biceps nodded. "Too long."

Tori flashed him a pointy-toothed smile. "Care to keep count of our kills, pretty boy?"

I wasn't sure what to make of these bounty hunters, but I wasn't surprised Kaalek was working with them. I pivoted to face him. "So, what's this about a plan?" I waved a hand at the others. "You ditch me the first chance you get but you have no problem fighting alongside them? From what I can tell, these two are just as female as I am."

His hands were braced on his hips, and he did not look happy with me. "*They* are not my responsibility."

"Neither am I," I snapped, matching his stance and dropping my voice. "And I'm definitely not your property."

He scowled and stepped closer to me. His eyes burned into me, making my legs wobble.

"I am the reason you are on this planet," he said, his voice deep and resonant and sending a rush of heat between my legs. "I need to keep you safe."

I hated how all I could think about was the way he'd felt inside me and how he'd made my body detonate like no one had before. Then I remembered that cold ache of loneliness when I'd woken up and he'd been gone. He would leave like they all did. I couldn't risk my heart for someone who could walk away from me. No matter how much it hurt to pull away from him.

I took a step back. "How many times do I have to tell you? I've been taking care of myself for most of my life. I don't need you to do it for me. I managed before you showed up, and I'll manage just fine once you're gone."

A muscle pulsed in his jaw and pain flickered in his gaze then was gone. "Fine." His angry expression was almost instantly replaced with one of cold indifference.

"Fine," I repeated, the chill of his gaze making me actually shiver.

"You two going to be able to work together, or should we put you in separate corners?" Tori asked, flipping the metal stick between her fingers.

"We're fine," I said, before he could speak. "Now what's the plan?"

CHAPTER TWENTY-NINE

Kaalek

I scowled at Tara as she crouched next to me, both of us waiting until the rest of the team was in place. This was exactly what I'd tried to prevent, but here she was, about to go into battle. Her curls were piled up on top of her head, and the coat Fenrey had made her helped her blend into the darkness, but she still seemed painfully small to me. I was used to being shoulder to shoulder with bulky and bare-chested Vandar raiders who could swing a battle axe as easily as they could breathe. Tara was not that.

Stubborn female, I thought. I hated how willful and impulsive she was, and how much she reminded me of myself.

At least she was by my side. She hadn't been pleased when I'd I insisted on being paired off with her—and the bounty hunters hadn't been so sure—but I'd been relentless. If she was with me, I could protect her. Even if she wouldn't admit it, she was mine to protect. Even more now that I'd claimed her, mating marks or not.

My usual mindset going into any fight was to kill as many of the enemy as possible. Victory over the empire had always been my only concern. That, and my reputation as a Raas to be feared. Now, I didn't care about either of those. No longer was winning and inflicting harm on my enemy enough. Those things had only left me empty and searching for more. Now, all I wanted was to pull off the attack, save the Carlogians, and keep Tara from getting hurt, which was proving to be easier said than done. Why was the one female I wanted to keep safe the same one who insisted on running headlong into danger?

My heart squeezed as I glanced down at her, a protective urge making me grip the hilt of my battle axe. Then I flashed back to tangling my hands in her fiery curls as she'd sucked me, and my cock twitched to life.

Tvek. I readjusted my swelling cock. This was not how I wanted to go into battle. I could not fight well if I was both preoccupied with keeping her safe and distracted by my desire to fuck her. But it was more than that, I realized as my stomach churned. I wanted more than to bury my cock in her. I wanted to *be* with her.

I glanced down at my chest. I could see a flash of my marks through the gap in the tunic. They were as they had always been. And would always be, I reminded myself. As much as I was drawn to the human and relished our sparring, she could never be more.

"We should go," she whispered to me, her gaze never leaving the single remaining guard at the entrance to the mine.

"Patience," I cautioned, snapping my mind away from my distracting thoughts. "We have not gotten the signal yet."

She shifted restlessly. "It won't be night for much longer."

I tilted my head to see the fading moons. The dark blue of the sky gave way to a lavender glow on the horizon, and the air was becoming noticeably warmer. A lone bird called out, as the sound of night insects quieted. Then there was the sharp click that did not come from any forest animal.

Tara grabbed my sleeve. "That's the signal. We should go."

I closed my hand over hers. "Tell me again what you will do."

She rolled her eyes. "Are you this nitpicky about every mission?" When I didn't answer or release her hand, she huffed out a breath. "Fine. I'm going to cover you as you approach the guard. If he spots you, I need to take him out with my blaster." She held up the blaster one of the bounty hunters had given her. "Once the guard is eliminated, I join you and we signal to the others."

I grunted an acknowledgement. It would have been much easier to keep her out of harm's way if she wasn't so capable. Tara was no weak female, and she refused to be treated like one. Why couldn't I have taken some simpering creature captive instead? One who would happily remain away from the battle and welcome me as a conquering hero?

Because you would be bored to tears, a little voice reminded me. As you were with all other females before Tara.

"Well?" Her green eyes narrowed at me. "Are you satisfied? Can we go, or do you need me to draw it in the dirt for you?"

I swatted her ass with my tail, and her mouth dropped open. "Did you just spank me? With your tail?"

"You talk too much," I said, loving the flush that appeared on her cheeks and that told me that she wasn't wholly upset by being spanked. "And I'm still in charge of this mission."

She pressed her lips together, shooting me daggers with her gaze. "As long as we're clear that it's all you're in charge of."

No, a simpering female would not have been nearly as exciting.

I focused my gaze on the mine entrance. "We'll see."

She opened her mouth to argue with me, but I held up my hand. "The guard is turning. It is time."

Without waiting for her to reply, I moved around the copse of trees and ran on my toes, closing the distance to the imperial guard in a matter of moments. Holding my battle axe high, I prepared to strike him down. Before I could reach him, he pivoted, swinging his laser rifle with him. His eyes widened, and he lifted the rifle quickly to aim at my chest.

He was faster than most imperial soldiers, and I spun to dodge the weapon fire. The heat of the laser did not sear the air as I expected because he dropped like a stone, hitting the ground and falling forward before I could bring my axe down across his back.

I looked over my shoulder and saw Tara striding from her hiding place, her blaster extended. "Did you...?" I stared down at the dead Zagrath soldier, his black helmet half off his head and a scorch mark darkening the blue of his uniform. "I was about to strike him down."

"You're welcome." She nudged the body with the toe of her boot. "Besides, he looked like he was going to get the drop on you."

My face warmed. "No imperial soldier has ever *gotten the drop on me*, as you say. If you'd waited, I would have struck him down."

She shrugged. "You should have figured out by now that I'm not good at waiting."

"Lokken is testing me," I muttered to myself, as Tara stripped the rifle off the dead soldier.

"Good work, you two." The human called Danica ran up to us, one of the gold aliens close on her heels. "We'll go into the mine while you cover us. Tori and Vrax are already clearing the barracks in the back."

"You should stay here," the alien with black slashes across his chest said to Danica. "It would be safer."

She shook her head, the stubborn set of her mouth a familiar sight. "I'm with you."

He put a hand over her belly. "You will be protecting more than me if you keep watch."

Her frown melted, and she gazed up at him with an expression I'd never seen. The moment was so intimate, I looked away. I saw that Tara shuffled her feet, her cheeks red and her gaze darting to the ground.

"I'll stay here, K'alvek," Danica said. "But you can't go alone."

K'alvek met my gaze, his eyes asking me without need of speech.

I gave him a single nod. "I will fight by your side."

He inclined his head at me in return, then placed a kiss on the human's brow and on her belly. "Stay safe."

I glanced at Tara, but her gaze was still on the ground. Part of me wanted to sweep her up into a kiss and another wanted to give her a hard swat with my tail. But I did neither, turning and following K'alvek through the arched entrance of the mine.

I would have to decide what to do with her soon—and with my own muddled feelings. But not now. Now was the time to kill some imperial soldiers and liberate the miners.

I drew in a breath of stale air and ran faster into the darkness, the alien warrior by my side.

CHAPTER THIRTY

Tara

I scanned the thick tree line, holding the Zagrath laser rifle in one hand and the blaster in the other. The sky was lightening faster now, a warm glow turning the sky pink and making it easier to see. I stole a glance at the woman next to me. "So, you and K'alvek…?"

Danica grinned and put a hand on her stomach. "He's not real subtle, is he?" She shook her head. "Dothveks aren't known for keeping secrets. Probably because they're empathic and don't believe in them."

Her smile was so infectious I couldn't help sharing it. "Congratulations. You seem happy."

She rubbed her belly again. "We are now, but it took a while for him to get the message that I didn't have any intention of changing my life just because we were together."

"I feel that," I said, my tone more grumbly than I'd intended.

"Yeah, I kind of got that from watching you and the Vandar."

I groaned. "It's that obvious?"

"I could light a fire from the sparks coming off you two," she said, nudging me. "I would have told you to get a room, but that doesn't seem to be an option out here."

I shook my head vigorously. "We definitely do *not* need to get a room. Or we shouldn't. It just mixes up everything. At least for me." I stopped when I realized I was babbling. "I don't know what's going on with us, but whatever it is, it can't go anywhere so I need to stop thinking about it. I need to stop thinking about *him*."

"Good luck with that," Danica said under her breath.

I swiveled my head to her. "You think I can't forget about him?"

"I don't know why it's so important to you that you do. It's obvious that there's something between you. Trust me, it's not worth trying to fight something that's real."

"Who says it's real?" I snapped, then immediately regretted my words. "I'm sorry. I don't mean to take out my frustration on you."

She patted my arm. "I get it. Big, tough aliens who are used to being in charge are a lot to handle. That doesn't mean it isn't worth it." She waggled her eyebrows. "And that Vandar is pretty gorgeous, especially if you like the dark, brooding type."

"He might be gorgeous, but he's also arrogant and bossy. I was the captain of my own ship. I've been taking care of myself for most of my life. I don't need some guy to come in and start going all alpha on me."

Danica tilted her head at me. "It's like listening to myself talk. I used to feel the exact same way you did."

"Really? What changed?"

She twitched up one shoulder. "Me? Him? Both of us? I guess we decided we were better together than apart."

I snorted out a laugh. "Kaalek and I are definitely not better together. We fight nonstop, and it takes every ounce of my self-control not to murder him."

"Sounds hot," she said with a wicked grin.

"You know, you're not helping." I turned back to survey the tree line with a frown. We were still supposed to be watching for incoming imperial soldiers and the bounty hunter captain wasn't helping diffuse my confusion.

"Sorry," she said, even though she didn't sound sorry. "All I'm saying is that before you decide there's no way it can work, maybe think about what it would be like if it did."

She pivoted back to face forward and we both stood in silence. I didn't want to think about what it would be like if things worked out with Kaalek—it wasn't a thought that had even remotely occurred to me—but once she'd said it, it was impossible *not* to think about it.

I readjusted my grip on the laser rifle. One thing I knew for sure, the sex would always be hot. I'd never been as turned on by anyone before in my life, and it wasn't just the freaky tail play. Even the way he kissed me made my body ignite, and his touch scorched my skin. I shivered just thinking about it.

Then I remembered how he looked at me—hot and possessive. Like I belonged to him. My heart beat faster at the thought of his claiming gaze, my body betraying me. I didn't belong to anyone, and I never would. As a Vandar raider, he might be used to taking what he wanted, but I wasn't something he could claim and keep.

Just keep telling yourself that, Tara.

And how would it work? Did he really expect me to give up my life to live with him on his warbird? I was used to commanding, not waiting around for the commander. I shook my head. I'd been too independent for too long to be a Vandar's whore. And I'd never be his mate. He'd told me as much when he'd talked about his mating marks. What had happened with my sister was unheard of and would not happen with us, especially since I wasn't like Astrid. I would never submit to Kaalek.

As the cold reality hit me, a knot formed in the pit of my stomach. Feelings didn't matter. I could never be his true mate, so there was no point in thinking about what could have been or what life might be like. Opening up to him any more than I had would only mean one thing. He would leave me, because sooner or later he would have to, and I would be alone again.

I bit the inside of my mouth until I tasted the tang of blood. My parents were gone, Astrid was gone, my crew was gone. I did not want to feel the same ache when Kaalek was gone.

Steeling myself, I focused on the mission at hand. I needed to help liberate the Carlogians, find a way to escape from the Vandar, and get back to my ship. Then life could resume, and I could forget about my brief affair with the Raas.

I blew out a breath, a calm already settling over me as I thought about resuming control of my ship. I might not be able to get my sister back, but I could sure as hell get my command back. And I'd feel better once I'd helped the Carlogians throw off the imperial rule. Fenrey and the other villagers deserved it, and I wasn't going to rest until the little tailor got his son back. I owed him that much.

A sharp nudge in my ribs snapped me out of my thoughts.

"Do you see that?" Danica whispered, her gaze fixed on the forest.

I squinted through the trees. Even though it wasn't dark anymore, the morning light was hazy, and a soft mist hung over the ground. Then I saw it. A flash of something shiny and black —something that didn't belong in a forest.

"Imperial soldiers!" I jerked her back into the entrance of the mine with me as laser fire erupted around us.

We both flattened ourselves on the sides of the arched entrance as red beams slashed through the air.

"Did you see how many?" Danica yelled over the noise as we stood side by side.

I shook my head. "Did you see where they came from? If those are the same soldiers I passed on my way here, that means they left the village."

"Maybe they figured out they'd been drawn away from the mine for a reason."

That made sense. Maybe the Zagrath weren't as stupid as I wanted them to be. "We can't let them get any closer. If they block the mine, we'll all be trapped inside." The idea of being trapped under the earth made me want to claw at my throat.

"Tori's still out there. She and Vrax will hear the weapons fire."

I nodded, but I knew that two against a squadron of well-armed, imperial soldiers wasn't great odds. I twisted my head to meet Danica's eyes. "Can you cover me?"

Before she could do more than bob her head up and down in shock, I pivoted around and started firing into the woods.

CHAPTER THIRTY-ONE

Kaalek

I heard the blasts before I could see them.

I'd taken the lead, with a row of Carlogians behind me and K'alvek bringing up the rear. It hadn't taken long to locate the miners and take out the guards watching them. As we'd suspected, most of the Zagrath had left the mines when the explosions had gone off in the village, so only a pair of soldiers had been watching the natives hack at the earth with rudimentary tools.

K'alvek had sliced one Zagrath guard across the throat, his curved blade proving to be every bit as deadly as I'd guessed. The other guard didn't so much as scream before I'd taken his head off with a single sweep of my battle axe. It had taken a little longer to explain to the miners that we were not attacking them, but once I'd mentioned Fenrey's name, a Carlogian who looked like a less wrinkled version of the tailor had rushed forward. His clothes were torn and dirty, but the workmanship was unmistakable and familiar.

"Your father and the Carlogian resistance sent us," I told him. "We are here to get you out."

He held out his hand, after wiping the dirt off on his equally filthy pants. "Lebben."

"Kaalek." I shook his hand, even though the custom struck me as strange.

Then the alien blinked his round eyes rapidly. "Did you say Carlogian resistance?"

It was clear he and his fellow villagers had been cut off from their people—and probably anything happening on the surface—since they'd been taken. "The remaining villagers have formed a resistance against the empire. It is because of them that we're here."

Lebben grinned. "That sounds like my father."

K'alvek cleared his throat. "We need to get you all out of here before the Zagrath realize what we're doing."

Lebben's grin faded and he nodded solemnly, getting the others into a line and helping us lead them up the steep and winding path to the top of the mine and the only way out. There were enough oil lamps hung on hooks along the way to keep the journey from being in total darkness, but not enough to fully light the tunnel. As a Vandar, I was used to low lighting and welcomed it, but I could tell the gold-skinned alien did not like the dark. I'd seen him cringe on the way down.

As we reached the top, morning light crept into the tunnel along with the sound of laser rifles. From the sounds of the blasts, it was clear that imperial reinforcements had arrived.

Fear gripped me as I thought about one thing only. Tara.

I clutched my battle axe as panic rippled through the miners behind me, their voices high with alarm.

K'alvek ran up to join me, his face grim. He knew what the

sounds meant, and his mate was also above in the firefight. We exchanged a silent look of steely resolve. We would get the Carlogians out and save our females—or we would go down fighting.

"Stay back," I ordered the group behind us without turning or slowing my pace. If they replied, I did not hear it over the rushing of blood in my ears. K'alvek ran beside me, his bare feet silent next to my pounding boots, and I welcomed the familiar feeling of fighting next to another warrior.

We burst out of the tunnel side by side with our blades high. It took a moment for us to assess the scene. Danica stood pressed up against one side of the arched entrance, one arm extended as she fired blindly into the forest. Her face was flushed, and she held one arm protectively across her belly.

K'alvek dove forward, shielding her with his body, taking the blaster from her, and continuing to fire.

It took me another moment to locate Tara. She was on the other side of the arch, crouched low and firing with her laser rifle, her expression determined. When I spotted her, I screamed her name.

She twisted to look at me, a smile curling her lips. "Took you long enough."

I glanced out into the forest to see a row of helmeted imperial soldiers advancing on the mine. We were easily outnumbered and definitely outgunned.

"We have to get everyone out of here," I called to K'alvek over the sound of the battle. "We can't let the miners get trapped below."

His slanted brows made a V between his eyes as he pressed them together. "Tori and Vrax should be here soon."

I'd almost forgotten about the Zevrian and his clansman clearing the barracks.

"While they provide a distraction," K'alvek said, "I will get our females to safety. You take the miners."

I didn't have long to wonder about the distraction. Soon, imperial soldiers were dropping to the ground and the hail of laser fire dwindled and then spluttered to a halt.

The Zevrian appeared from the side, blasters in both hands. She'd managed to flank the Zagrath while they'd been focused on shooting at us.

"They're down," she yelled, jogging over to us and eyeing the human tucked behind K'alvek. "You good, Captain?"

The human pushed past K'alvek, looking annoyed. "I'm fine and not breakable, like some people seem to think."

K'alvek didn't appear even slightly bothered by this outburst. I found myself liking this Dothvek more all the time.

I turned to Tara, who was straightening from her hunched position. Before I could ask her if she was okay and assuredly get a sharp response, a blast of red exploded across her chest and she flew backward, landing hard on her back. The Zevrian whirled and fired in the direction of the blast while the human captain screamed and ran to Tara's motionless form.

Time seemed to slow to a crawl as I watched her bend over Tara, whose arms were sprawled unnaturally out to her side. K'alvek bellowed something to me, but his voice sounded like it was far away. The only thing I saw was the imperial fighter who hadn't been killed and who'd pushed himself up from the ground to fire.

The Zevrian clipped him in the shoulder, and he went down again. Rage stormed through me hot and fast, as I put a hand on her arm, shaking my head while she prepared to fire again. "Let me."

I stalked past her and through the undergrowth, catching the coward as he attempted to crawl away. I ripped off his helmet and was rewarded with a scream. I did not wait to see what damage I'd inflicted. I grasped a handful of his hair, jerking his head back and separating it from his body with a slice of my axe blade.

I stood over his body, heaving and holding the head. Only then did the sounds start rushing back to me—the Zevrian cursing, Danica trying to rouse Tara, and the distressed chattering of the natives as they swarmed from the mine and the barracks.

Lifting my gaze to where Tara still lay, I dropped the Zagrath head and walked back. The rage drained from me and grief poured in, as I took agonizing steps to reach her. The human glanced up when I stood over Tara, her face streaked with tears. She moved away without a word, and I dropped to my knees.

I picked up Tara, her body light in my arms. Her flame-colored waves cascaded behind her, and her eyes were closed. It was wrong to feel so much sorrow for someone I had only known for such a short time. It made no sense.

Vandar did not mourn death. We celebrated it. A valiant warrior would spend eternity in Zedna with Lokken and the other gods of old. It was an afterlife we anticipated with great joy.

I looked on Tara's pale cheeks. But she was not Vandar. She was not a warrior, and she had not been my mate. She would not be waiting for me in Zedna when I reached the gates after a valiant battle.

I would never see the stubborn, aggravating human again. I would never argue with her. She would never drive me to the point where I wished I could put her out an air lock. I stroked a finger down the side of her face. I would never get the chance to see if she could be something more to me—if she could truly be mine.

I'd known the possibility of a human taking my mating marks had been slim, but it had been there. There had been the chance—the faintest hope flickering in the back of my mind. A hope that was now gone.

I pulled her to me, burying my head in her hair and inhaling the scent of her, desperate to imprint it in my brain. "I am sorry, Tara."

A puff of warm breath on my neck made me almost drop her. I jerked back, gaping down as she blinked up at me.

"I get shot and all you can do is smell my hair and tell me you're sorry?"

CHAPTER THIRTY-TWO

Tara

Kaalek crushed me to his chest again, his breath hitching unevenly.

"Okay, okay," I said, drawing in my own breath, my ribs aching. "I get it. You're happy to see me."

He finally loosened his grip on me, lowering me to the ground. "How is this possible? I saw the laser strike you in the chest."

I peered down at myself. The black coat Fenrey had made me now wore a large scorch mark on one side, but there were no holes. I touched the fabric, which was warm. "I think Fenrey made me a laser-proof coat."

Kaalek's eyes raked over the fabric, and he ran his fingers across it. "These Carlogians continue to impress me."

I pressed a palm to his own tunic. "It's the same fabric. He made us both armored clothing." I peered up at him, focusing on the pained expression on his face. "Why are you sorry?"

"What?"

"You whispered that you were sorry when you thought I was dead. Why were you so sorry? I mean, I can think of a few things, but I didn't think Vandar did regrets—or apologies."

He cleared his throat before opening his mouth, his eyes searching mine.

"She's alive?" Danica cried as she bent down next to Kaalek, her gaze skittering over me. "But you were...I saw you..."

Kaalek released me and pulled away as Danica fussed over me. Whatever he'd been about to tell me would have to wait.

I pointed to my coat. "Laser-proof clothes."

Her eyebrows went skyward. "Seriously? You'll have to tell me where you got that."

I pushed myself so I was sitting up without being supported. Although the impact had knocked me out and my ribs ached from the laser-fire, I was regaining my strength quickly. "We should get back to the village. When I left, the resistance was hiding in the tunnel, but Fenrey stayed up top to close the hatch."

Kaalek's expression hardened. "You're right. This battle is not yet won."

Danica stood and helped pull me up. "We'll help you get these miners back to their village." She glanced over her shoulder at the Carlogians gathered behind us. Their clothes were dirty and even their striped horns were covered in dust. The ones who'd been underground were shielding their eyes from the morning light, although it was diffused through the trees.

The pair of gold-skinned aliens were walking among the bodies of the Zagrath soldiers, poking at them with their feet. I was glad they were making sure the enemy was truly dead this time.

"We've got all the natives," Tori said, her hair back to being piled on her head with the two metal sticks holding it in place.

"The barracks are cleared, and the guards handled." The menacing quirk of her lips left no mystery as to what she meant by that.

"How far is the village?" Danica asked, eyeing the dirt path cutting through the woods.

"Not far if we run," Kaalek told her.

Easy for him to say, I thought. The Raas had long legs, as did the gold aliens. And none of them had just been shot. Not that I was going to complain. Not after I'd made such a big deal about being a captain who should be treated as an equal.

One of the Carlogians stepped forward. Although he was younger, he reminded me of Fenrey. He beckoned the other natives with a wide sweep of his arm. "Come on. We know the way."

They all started running toward the village, some loping along and some kicking up dust behind them.

Danica's mate strode over to her and scooped her up without asking, then took off running with the pack of Carlogians. The other alien took a step toward Tori, but she bared her pointy teeth at him.

"Don't even think about it, pretty boy."

He half smiled, half growled at her, then they both started to run.

"We'll bring up the rear." Kaalek walked to me and scooped me up, much like Danica's mate had done. I started to complain, but he gave me a severe look. "You have just been shot. If you argue with me about this, I will throw you over my shoulder."

I attempted to match his severe expression, but I was too relieved and weary to pull it off. "Fine, but don't think this is going to happen all the time."

He started to run, careful not to jostle me. "I would never think that."

He was mocking me, but I just scowled at his quivering lips and hooked my arm around his neck. I didn't have the strength yet to run. I probably didn't even have the energy to keep up with the slowest Carlogian—a skinny fellow that Kaalek had to slow down not to blow past.

I leaned my head against his chest. Even covered in the fabric of his tunic, his solid muscle was comforting. I tried not to think too much about how good it had felt when I'd been curled up next to him in bed. I needed to stop thinking about how much I liked that. I had to put that out of my mind if I was going to go back to captaining my own ship.

"You are sure you were not injured?" he asked, as he jogged at a steady pace next to the slowest Carlogian.

"It stunned me, but the fabric absorbed most of the hit."

He nodded, pain contorting his handsome features for a brief moment. "I owe Fenrey a great debt. I do not know what..." He jerked his gaze away from me, staring out at the path and clenching his jaw.

"Kaalek?"

He did not look down again, but his face was stormy. I wanted to ask him what he'd meant by that, but I was almost afraid of the answer.

Then the sounds of screaming tore through the air, and his grip on me loosened. The Carlogians running in front of us stopped suddenly then dashed into the forest as laser fire hit the ground around us.

Kaalek dove for cover, landing in the underbrush, tucking me into his chest, and rolling through leaves and crawling vines until we came to a stop with him lying on top of me.

I couldn't see a thing, but it was clear from the sounds of weapons being fired that we were under attack.

"What's happening?" I asked, craning my neck back to get a glimpse. I twisted my neck to one side and saw some of the Carlogians huddled near us, their arms over their heads.

"Ambush," Kaalek said, then he spat out the last word. "Zagrath."

"Fuck. Where did all they come from?"

He jerked his chin up. "The sky."

I craned my head around his and saw that he was right. Gunmetal-gray ships hovered above the forest, shooting into the trees. This was not good. "They called for reinforcements."

Kaalek nodded, his lips a hard, white line.

My stomach lurched. "They're going to go after the village." I tried to push him off me. "We have to help them."

Kaalek held me under him as I struggled. "I can't let you go."

I slapped at his arms. "Is this more of that captive bullshit? I'm not trying to get away from you, you big lug. I'm trying to help our friends."

"You risking your life won't help them."

I tried to knee him, but his legs were too heavy pressed against mine. "I have to try. Let me up!"

His eyes were wild, as explosions shook the ground around us, and dirt flew into the air. He grabbed the sides of my head and held it so that our faces were nearly touching. "I can't lose you again," he yelled. "I'd rather die myself!"

CHAPTER THIRTY-THREE

Kaalek

Tara's body went still beneath me, and she blinked rapidly as she gazed up at me. Laser fire shattered the air and the earth trembled, but all I could hear was her sharp intake of breath.

"What did you say?"

"I can't risk you getting hurt," I said, forcing the words out even as my throat was thick with emotion. "When I thought you died, I wanted to die myself. I can't lose you."

I didn't wait for her to respond before crushing my lips to hers. I'd wanted to kiss her since she'd come back to life in my arms, and I couldn't hold back any longer. I needed to taste her and feel her and prove to myself that she was truly alive.

Her lips were as soft as I remembered but they moved hungrily against mine. She was just as eager as I was, her tongue tangling with mine, as she wrapped her arms around my neck and moaned into my mouth.

Heat stormed through my body and my cock hardened, straining in my pants. Need throbbed like a heartbeat as I kissed her deeply, savoring the sweetness of her mouth and desperate noises she made. The rumbling of the ground forced me to tear my lips from her. We were both breathing as if we'd been running a race, and her cheeks were flushed.

Tara's eyes were heavy with desire, and she gave a small shake of her head as if shaking off a daze. "I thought I drove you crazy and annoyed you."

"You do."

Her look of shock became a scowl then the corners of her mouth quivered. "Well, right back at you."

I cocked my head at her, confused by her words.

"It means, I feel the same way about you. You annoy the hell out of me most of the time, but I'd rather be with you and annoyed than apart from you."

I kissed her again as happiness swelled within me. "You don't want to escape from me?"

She smirked at me. "Not *all* the time."

I brushed a curl off her forehead. "I know it's wrong to want you to stay with me when we can never—"

"You know I don't buy all that destiny crap, right?" She put a hand to the side of my face. "The only thing I believe in is right now. And right now, I'm happy being with you. Even though I do want to kill you most of the time."

I released a breath. "I am happy with you." It still gnawed at me that she would not wear my mating marks, but I refused to let that ruin the moment.

She swatted my chest. "But why the hell did you wait until we were under attack to tell me? This was about the least romantic time you could have picked."

"Romantic?"

She shook her head. "I guess the Vandar don't do romance."

I wasn't even sure what it meant to be romantic, but I was pretty sure it didn't mean me screwing her in the woods as the empire fired around us.

I swiveled my head. The Carlogians were still cowering around us as the Zagrath fired from above. At least the forest was thick enough that they couldn't see through it, so their laser fire was random and focused mainly on the dirt path.

"They're trying to keep us from the road," I said, pushing myself off Tara.

"Well, they're doing a great job."

I rolled onto my hands and knees. "If we stay low and keep to the trees, we should be able to keep running."

She didn't look convinced.

"You wanted to get to the village," I reminded her, as I got into a crouch and took her hand. "Just stay close to me."

She set her jaw and gave me a sharp nod. "Let's do it."

We moved forward and the Carlogians followed suit, some scrabbling on all fours and others running hunched over. I looped an arm around Tara and held her to my side, the warmth of her body reassuring me. We were still far away from the tunnel opening, if I could even locate it again in the chaos of the shooting.

Up ahead, I spotted the Zevrian. A band of cloth was tied around her arm and the gold-skinned alien who was obviously with her scowled as he adjusted it.

"She got hit," he said, as we approached.

She rolled her eyes at him. "It's a scratch."

"If we keep to the forest, the imperial ships have less of a chance of spotting us," I told them.

As we continued our procession, the crashing of trees was followed by a loud thud from behind. We all turned as an imperial shuttle set down on the dirt path where we'd been, a few felled trees surrounding it.

Tvek. As soon as that ramp lowered, soldiers would be swarming through the woods.

"Run!" Tara screamed, causing the Carlogians to give up their crouched positions and begin tearing through the woods.

The Zevrian met my eyes, and I recognized the steely resolve. She wasn't running. The alien next to her also squared his shoulders and faced the imperial ship. Neither of them were.

I grasped Tara by the shoulders and locked eyes with her. "I need you to get these people to their village. I'll meet you there."

"As if." She jerked out of my grasp and stood next to me.

I opened my mouth to argue with her, but she waved a hand.

"As your people say, it is done." She leveled a blaster at the ship. "But don't even think of getting killed, Kaalek. I will *so* kick your ass if you do."

I held my battle axe in a defensive position, my gaze on the enemy ship. "I wouldn't dream of it."

The laser fire from above had ceased, and I held my breath as I waited for the sound of boots pounding down the metal ramp. But before the ramp touched down there was a burst of hot air and another heavy thud, dirt kicking up on the path near us.

My pulse quickened as a Vandar ship materialized, the ramp opening and bare-chested warriors pouring out from within. Another Vandar shuttle appeared on the other side of the imperial shuttle, warriors swarming the enemy ship as the soldiers emerged and were quickly cut down.

"Is that...?" Tara said.

Pride welled in my chest. "My horde." I flicked my gaze to her. "Stay here. I'll be right back."

I leapt forward without waiting for her arguments. Blood rushed in my ears as I ran headlong into the fray, dodging blaster fire and cutting down the few remaining Zagrath soldiers staggering out of the shuttle. When I spun around, my battle axe dripping blood, I saw my *majak* heaving in ragged breaths.

He spotted me and grinned. "I hope we were not too late, Raas."

CHAPTER THIRTY-FOUR

Kaalek

"Jorl!" I ran to him, pounding him on the shoulder when I reached him. "You picked up the emergency beacon?"

"We detected no homing beacon."

Then the Zagrath *had* disabled it when they'd found my crashed ship. "But you still found us."

He looked at me, then pushed a dark braid off his shoulder. "You thought we would not? I know your mind, Kaalek. It was not hard to deduce what had happened and where you would have gone—once we determined you were not at the rendezvous point."

I was so pleased to see him and all my warriors that I thumped his shoulder again. "Which is why you are my *majak*."

He twisted his head to take in the scene. "And the female? Did she escape?"

"She is here somewhere." I swiveled around to look for her.

The grin on Jorl's face slipped. "The female is not being guarded?"

"She will not run from me," I said, not sure how much I should share with my *majak*. Even though he was my most trusted warrior, he would not understand my attachment to the human.

"Then you must have tied her up well," my battle chief, Symdar, said as he joined us. He wiped the back of his hand across his forehead, smearing blood that was not his. "I saw the scars and bruises she gave both you and Jorl."

"Kaalek!" Tara ran up to me, throwing her arms around my waist. She seemed to realize that my warriors were gaping at her, so she twisted her head around to smile at them. "Hi, guys. Thanks for flying in and saving the day. Kaalek and I were almost goners."

Jorl blinked at her without speaking.

She pointed to the faded slash across his cheek. "Looks like the cut I gave you is healing well. Sorry about that, by the way. I'm not a big fan of being told what to do."

Symdar was the first to recover himself, clearing his throat and giving her a curt nod. "I am glad to see you are unharmed."

Tara peered up at me and lowered her voice to a conspiratorial whisper. "So, it's not just you who has a way with words."

"Raas?" Jorl asked, the emphasis on the word imparting every question he had.

"Tara is no longer a prisoner of the Vandar," I said. "She is free is go as she pleases, but she is also welcome to stay on my ship as a guest."

"A guest?" Jorl looked at me as if I'd suggested we bring a pride of flesh-eating *nurly-cats* onto the warbird. "Raas, the Vandar almost never take captives, and even more rarely have guests."

"That is true." I wrapped one arm around Tara. "But I am

Raas, am I not? I have the right to say what happens on my warbird and in my horde."

Jorl dropped his gaze. "Of course, Raas. I was only—"

"Your counsel is appreciated, *majak*. But now, we should turn our attention to the Carlogian village."

"More imperial soldiers to kill?" Symdar asked, spinning the handle of his battle axe, the blade glinting as it caught the light.

I shook my head. "Carlogians to save. The villagers formed an underground resistance to the Zagrath. They are the ones who helped us draw the soldiers from the mine with carefully planned acts of sabotage. They need our aid."

Symdar's expression drooped for a moment, but he clicked his heels sharply. "Yes, Raas."

Jorl indicated a nearby transport with a nod of his head. "This will be faster."

I swept my gaze quickly around us. Fallen Zagrath littered the ground, and Vandar warriors prowled the perimeter with their axes dripping red as they divested the dead fighters of their weapons. Blood mixed with dirt beneath the bodies, the scent familiar and distinctive in my nose. The enemy hadn't stood a chance against my well-trained and menacing warriors.

It was almost comforting to be surrounded by the remnants of battle, although it did not give me the same rush that it usually did. What made my pulse quicken was the female I held to my side.

"The Carlogians kept running," Tara said, when I looked away from the carnage. "I told them to go ahead without me. " She pressed a hand to my chest. "You know I'm no good at taking orders. Besides, if you were going to die fighting, then so was I."

I shook my head, even as my heart swelled with affection for the stubborn female. "A Raas and a captain are both used to leading. This does not seem like a good idea."

She winked at me, then tugged me toward the transport ship. "Fun, right?"

Symdar and Jorl exchanged a shocked look that was not lost on me.

"The human will not have a position of authority on our ship, will she, Raas?" Jorl asked, his hushed tone incredulous.

I gave a curt shake of my head as Tara walked ahead of me. "I am still Raas."

His eyes darted to my chest, which was covered by the long tunic. "Does she share your—?"

"She does not," I growled, displeased that his question caused such sudden pain. I hated to be reminded that the human female was not Vandar, and would most likely never share my mating marks. If I ever wished for a legacy, I would not be able to keep Tara as my mate, and she could never become my Raisa. I had never even uttered the word around her—its existence taunted me with what would never be.

I shook those thoughts away. I did not care about that now. All that mattered was Tara. I liked the way she made me feel, and I liked who I was when I was around her. When she was not exasperating me to the point of madness, she was challenging me to be better.

Since we'd been on the planet, she'd cracked open a part of my heart I'd thought had been locked away forever. She'd awoken my compassion and tamped down my desire for vengeance. My blood did not run hot all the time for revenge against the empire. Now it ran hot with passion for her.

I stomped up the ramp of the transport, grasping an overhead bar and circling an arm and my tail around Tara to keep her steady as the ship's engines rumbled. She swayed as we lifted off, leaning her small body against mine for balance.

Jorl met my eyes over her head and cocked an eyebrow. It was a look of curiosity, not judgment. He did not understand what had happened between us, but he would have my back. If

Tara was to be part of our crew, he would defend her life with as much dedication as he did mine. This I knew without question.

"Raas," he said over the hum of the ship as we skimmed above the trees. "You should know that the empire does not seem inclined to let this planet go without a bloody battle."

"They need the rare minerals that are beneath the planet's surface," I told him. "It is what they mined for, and why they will not go easily."

"They have amassed many ships around the planet," Symdar added. "Battleships we have never seen before. Our horde is fighting them off as we speak."

I looked from one warrior to the other. "You think we are outmatched?"

Jorl hesitated before shaking his head. "Not anymore." He met my eyes and held them. "Since you were missing, I had to make command decisions that were in the best interest of the horde and the planet."

"As I would have expected," I said, shifting as the transport touched down at the far end of the village. "There is no one I would trust with those decisions more, *majak*."

Jorl released a breath. "I am glad to hear you say that, Raas."

The ramp of the transport lowered to reveal more Vandar ships around the village, and more warriors prowling around the houses and shops lining the central road. I narrowed my gaze. But not all my warriors.

"You called for another horde to assist?" I asked, my breath catching as I recognized the Vandar taking purposeful steps toward us. His black hair fluttered as he walked, and a leather strap cut across his chest and the swirling mating marks that covered his chest, stomach, and arms.

I rapped my fingers across the hilt of my axe as my stomach tightened as it always did when I saw him.

Kratos. My elder brother.

CHAPTER THIRTY-FIVE

Tara

Kaalek stiffened behind me, and I followed his gaze out of the ship. I spotted the bounty hunters who'd helped us at the mine, and the miners we'd rescued as they were joyfully reunited with their family and friends. Then I saw the huge Vandar walking toward us. "Who is that?"

"Kratos."

I whipped my head up. "As in, your brother? The guy who took Astrid?" I looked back at him, recognizing the shoulder armor from when he'd boarded my freighter. "He looks a lot less scary now."

Kaalek choked back a laugh. "Do not be fooled. He was trained by our father, and there was not a more brutal Raas."

His voice was low, but emotion hung thick in it. One thing was clear. Kaalek had no love lost for his father.

"So, he's here to…?" I asked.

"Offer assistance from one Raas to another," Kaalek said,

his tone now stripped of all feeling. He uncoiled his tail from my legs and dropped his hand from my waist. "I should greet him."

Without another word, he walked off the ship and met his brother near the village square. The two Vandar raiders faced off, their similarities so striking I was glad they were dressed differently so I could tell them apart.

Kaalek was almost the match for his brother in height and size, although he was younger, and both wore their straight, black hair long and loose. Even the way they held themselves was striking—hands clasped behind their backs and heads tilted slightly.

I waited until they'd had a chance to speak a few words to each other before I decided I'd waited long enough. I pushed past Kaalek's *majak* and battle chief, hurrying toward the two Raases before either warrior could think to stop me.

Kratos faced me, nodding as Kaalek spoke. His eyes shifted to me as I approached, then widened slightly.

Good, I thought. He remembered me.

Kratos glanced back at his brother as I reached them. "You found the freighter, I see."

Kaalek looked down at me, scowling and finally shaking his head in obvious frustration. "Yes, although it was not as easy to neutralize the situation as I'd hoped."

Kratos let his gaze drift from me to Kaalek. Then he barked out a laugh. "I could have warned you, brother."

"I did not need your advice," Kaalek spat out, then looked back at me and shook his head. "Maybe I did."

"You have achieved much as a Raas without it," Kratos said. "You have never needed my counsel, but it has always been here if you wanted it. I have always been here, even if our father was not."

Kaalek locked eyes with him and something passed between the two Vandar. He cleared his throat, nodding brusquely.

"What do you remember of him?" Kratos asked, shifting as he stood.

"Not much. Mostly him leaving."

Kaalek's older brother let out a bitter laugh. "He excelled at that. And killing. But not at being a father—to either of us."

Kaalek's shoulders sank noticeably. "It was hard being his apprentice, wasn't it?"

"I would not have wished it on you, brother."

The two Vandar held each other's gaze for a moment then Kratos cut his eyes to me quickly and returned his gaze to his brother, one eyebrow quirking. "It appears it is done."

"As much as it can be," Kaalek said, shifting his body closer to me.

I put my hands on my hips and gave Kratos my most ferocious glare. "As fun as it is to be talked about when I'm standing right in front of you, I want to know where my sister is."

"She is well," he said.

I cocked an eyebrow at him. "You're kidding, right? That's all I get? She is well? Pardon me for not trusting the guy who forced her off my ship, but I want to see her." I pointed a finger at the ground. "Right here. Right now."

The edges of the Raas' mouth quivered, and he glanced at his brother. "It seems you will never be bored, brother."

"No," Kaalek said with a tortured sigh. "That will not be my problem."

I swung to face Kaalek. "Is this a joke to you two? I swear to—"

"Tara!"

The sound of Astrid's voice made the words die on my lips. I looked past Kratos and saw her descending from a black, winged ship next to what appeared to be a child-sized raider. If I hadn't heard her speak, I might not have known it was her.

She wore what looked like a Vandar battle kilt, but with matching leather leggings underneath and boots laced halfway up her calves. A black vest looked molded to her skin, dark swirls extending down her bare arms and peeking from the V-neck. Her blonde hair was pulled up into a high bun, making her features striking. This badass woman taking purposeful steps toward me looked nothing like the shy, unsure girl I'd known who'd hidden behind her hair and hummed to calm herself.

"Astrid?" My voice cracked.

She broke into a run, smiling broadly. The smile I recognized. I took off running myself, meeting her and almost falling over when she tackled me in a hug. Although she was shorter than me and had always been more timid, her hug was anything but.

"I'm so happy to see you," she said, squeezing her arms around me.

It was hard for me to talk, but I nodded as I fought back tears. I finally held her at arm's length. "What happened to you? You look so different."

She smiled, her gaze sliding past me to rest on Kratos. "I'm happy, Tara. Really, truly happy."

I gave her shoulders a quick shake and pulled her gaze back to me. "Are you sure? He's treating you well?"

"Yes, he's treating me very well." She laughed as I gaped at her. "Don't look so surprised. Raas Kratos is not what they all say about him."

"I hope not," I muttered, although I'd learned that Raas Kaalek wasn't quite the brute he liked others to think he was either. "And you want to stay on his ship? With him?" I lowered my voice to a whisper. "He's not forcing you?"

"The Raas would never do that." The high voice from below drew my gaze down to the boy I'd seen descend from the ship next to my sister. He had dark hair and a ferocious expression on his boyish face as he held the hilt of his blade tightly.

"It's okay, Krin." Astrid put an arm on his shoulder. "Why

don't you go check out the village while I talk to my sister? But don't go too far."

"If you're sure." The boy gave me some serious side eye before backing away.

"And that is...?' I asked once he'd moved far enough away not to hear. "I know you haven't been gone long enough to have a kid."

She laughed. "One of the Vandar apprentices who's become my friend."

I spotted the boy lingering close enough to keep one eye on Astrid. "I think you mean your shadow."

"He's very loyal. Just like his Raas."

I made a noise in the back of my throat. "He's not making you say that?"

She tilted her head at me. "I'm not as easily persuaded as I once was, Tara."

I noticed the confidant glint in her eyes. "I can see that."

"Besides," she added, sending Kratos another tender look, "he wouldn't want to force me to do or say anything."

My gaze went to the marks curling across her skin. "I guess I believe you, since you actually got his mating marks." For some strange reason, seeing them made my heart clench, and I experienced a rush of something I'd never experienced when it came to my younger sister—jealousy.

She touched a hand to her throat. "To be honest, it freaked me out at first—and the burning sensation wasn't fun—but then it was pretty cool. No human has ever gotten them before."

I nodded, my throat tight. "They look good on you." It was true. They looked right on her, as if she'd always been destined to have them and to be dressed like a Vandar warrior. "And you're truly happy living on a raider warbird?"

She squeezed my hand. "Truly."

I let my shoulders relax. "As long as you're happy and he

deserves you. I wouldn't be able to rest if I knew you weren't okay."

"Always the big sister." She gave me a knowing grin. "So, now that we've determined that I'm fine, do you want to tell me what you're doing with Kratos' younger brother?"

I didn't turn around, even though I wanted to sneak a look at him. Instead, I let out a huff. "He came after my ship as payback for me sending the empire after you. I guess these hordes don't like it when you work with the Zagrath."

"You didn't get that the first time we were boarded?" Her tone of voice made her sound like the older and wiser one.

I tapped a foot on the handpicked earth. "You didn't expect me to not try to find you, did you?"

"I guess not. I'm just glad they didn't blow up your ship."

"That's how I ended up with Kaalek. I bargained with him to leave the ship alone. If I went with him, he wouldn't blow it up. Since the crew was hiding in all the smugglers' hidey holes, it was a deal I had to make."

"Sounds like the Tara I know." She eyed me. "But you don't look like you're an unwilling prisoner."

My cheeks warmed. "I guess Raas Kaalek isn't what I expected him to be, either."

Astrid threw an arm around my shoulders. "That's what I hoped you'd say. Now, before we have to go, I want to hear all the details."

I gave her a scandalized look. "Since when do you want to exchange sordid stories?"

She giggled and dropped her voice. "Since I actually have some to share." She walked us away from the pair of Vandar. "Now spill the dirt about the younger one. Is he as wild and impulsive as his brother says he is?"

CHAPTER THIRTY-SIX

Kaalek

After we'd gotten word from the hordes above the planet that the imperial ships were in retreat, the bounty hunters had wished us farewell and taken off with the female captain hugging Tara hard and telling her she'd always have a job on their ship. Then Kratos and his mate had reluctantly said their goodbyes.

My older brother had pulled me into a one-armed embrace before he'd boarded his transport, reminding me to contact him if I needed advice about handling a human. Tara had held her sister for so long I'd thought they might never let go, but then she'd released her and walked away before the ship had lifted off the ground, heading to Fenrey's shop and disappearing behind the door.

I hesitated to follow her. We'd seen Fenrey's tearful reunion with his son. I did not relish interrupting his private time or telling Tara that we needed to go. Even after what we'd admitted to each other, I was not sure she still wished to remain with me.

I'd seen the look on her face when she'd noticed her sister's mating marks. Her gaze had been drawn to them again and again as they'd talked. Did it bother her that we did not share them? Did it make what we had less real?

For the first time in my life, I cursed Vandar traditions as I made my way to the tailor's shop, my flesh prickling as anger bubbled up inside me. I took a breath to temper myself and held my hand over the wooden door before knocking. Before I could calm myself enough to knock, though, the door swung open.

Fenrey looked startled, then pleased to see me. "Just the warlord I was looking for."

"I wanted to tell you that the empire is in retreat. We cannot guarantee that they will never return, but you now have two Vandar hordes ready and willing to offer you aid if they ever do. I know you hate the Zagrath technology, but we left the local imperial transmission station intact so you could contact us in case of an emergency. It will also transmit a Vandar signal that should give the empire pause."

"Yes, yes." He pulled me inside. "That's all very good." He stole a glance over his shoulder. "But what are you going to do about Tara?"

"Did you hear what I said about the empire?"

He frowned at me. "Life is not always about the big events, you know. That's not to say we aren't grateful to all the Vandar for saving us and for bringing my son back to me." He pressed a hand to his ascot. "But I can't bear to see the human so unhappy."

"She's unhappy?"

He shrugged. "I might be an old man, but I know what it looks like when a female is not happy." He tugged me toward the back of his shop. "You need to tell her that you love her."

The word pulled me up short. "Love?"

He groaned. "Yes, love. I've seen the way you look at each other. Again, I'm old. Not blind."

"But I told her that I wanted her to—"

He waved a hand at me as he pulled me through the heavy curtain over the door. "Whatever you told her wasn't enough."

I stopped when we reached the kitchen. "Did she say something to you?"

He shook his head. "She didn't have to. I was bonded to my mate for over sixty rotations. I know what I'm talking about." He rolled back the rug and jerked up the hatch. "She's down there, gathering her things. I'll close this after you, so you'll have privacy. The rest of the resistance is outside celebrating, anyway." He prodded me toward the ladder. "Now go fix things."

I backed down the ladder, not knowing how I was supposed to fix things. I didn't understand females, and especially not human ones. I'd given her everything I could. Without mating marks, I couldn't take her as a true mate, and I refused to lie to her and say I could.

I scratched at my chest as I reached the bottom of the ladder, the laser-proof fabric of the tunic finally proving to be irritating. I would be glad to be out of the Carlogian clothes and back in my Vandar battle kilt.

"Are they gone?" Tara asked as she came out of the secret room, the coat Fenrey had made her tucked under one arm.

"They are." I noticed that she didn't meet my eyes, as she rubbed a hand at the base of her neck. "*Vaes*. It's time to return to our ship?"

She bit her bottom lip, rubbing her throat harder. "About that."

"You do not wish to remain with me," I said, knowing that she'd changed her mind before she even told me.

She finally lifted her gaze to mine. "It's just that seeing Astrid reminded me that you can never really be with someone who doesn't have your mating marks, and I'm not the type of woman to hang around if I know it isn't going anywhere. Not with you, at least."

Her cheeks were splotched with red, and when she removed her hand I saw that the flush even mottled her chest, a sharp contrast to the inky line curling up from underneath her vest. I stopped breathing for a moment as I realized what I was seeing. I ripped open my tunic, staring down at the skin that I'd thought had been itching. My own marks were extending across my skin and down my arms.

"What are you doing?" She stepped back from me, looking at me like I'd lost my mind.

I swept her up into my arms as she screamed and slapped at me.

When I put her down again, I reached over and ripped open her vest, almost crying out loud when I saw my own mating marks reflected on her ivory skin.

"Are you insane?" She yanked her vest closed. "I just told you that I don't—"

"Mating marks," I said, taking her chin in my hand and forcing her to meet my eyes. "You have my mating marks, Tara."

For a moment, I thought she hadn't understood me. Then she looked down, opening her vest and gasping. She looked up at me, her eyes sparkling. "I didn't think it was possible."

"Did you not think I loved you as madly as Kratos loves your sister?"

If it was possible for her jaw to drop open farther, it did. "Did you say you love me?"

Instead of answering her with words, I crushed my mouth to hers, backing her up against the wall of the tunnel. I needed to feel her, to be inside her, to claim my true mate.

She moaned into the kiss, her hands moving as frantically as mine. I cupped her breasts in my hands, thumbing her nipples as the flesh pebbled beneath my fingers then moving one hand farther down to yank at her pants. Without breaking the kiss, she tugged my pants down until my cock sprang free, fisting it in one hand and causing a rumble to escape from my throat.

I could barely control myself as I pressed her hard into the wall, and she moved one hand along my shaft. She tore her mouth from mine, her hot gaze burning into me.

"Yes, Tara. I said love. Can't you see that you're my true mate?"

She laughed as her eyes glittered bright. "I love you, too. I shouldn't because you're still an arrogant ass sometimes, but I do."

"And you are no less impossible than you have always been."

"Kaalek." Her voice was breathy, and her eyes locked on mine and narrowed. "I need you inside me."

"This is one time I will not argue with you, mate." I pulled her pants down over her ass, and she kicked them off the rest of the way. I lifted her so that her legs were wrapped around my waist, and my cock was notched at her entrance.

"You're so wet for me already," I said, my heart hammering in my chest.

She nodded, her eyes half-lidded with desire as I lowered her onto my cock. My own vision clouded as her tight heat enveloped me. I thrust up and held myself deep. "Is that what you wanted?"

Tara's eyelids fluttered. "Yes, Kaalek."

"You are mine now." I gripped her hips and moved her up and down my shaft. "Say it."

She looked dazed as she nodded.

I moved away from the wall and shifted my hands to her round ass. "Say it, Tara. You are my mate."

"I'm yours," she gasped, her eyes wild. "I only want you, Kaalek."

I groaned from the pleasure of her wet heat clenching me.

"This is mine now." I drove her down harder. "You are mine. No one else will ever fuck you but me."

Her molten eyes held mine. "Yes, Raas."

Hearing her call me Raas made me pound her up and down even harder, her cries echoing through the tunnel. I brought my tail up to rub against her slick nub, as she tipped over the edge, and her body rippled around me. With a final guttural sound as she screamed her release, I drove her down and pulsed into her. She arched back and scratched at my shoulders, finally sagging into me, her arms trembling.

Leaning against the wall again, I held her legs around my waist even as my own shook. The roaring in my ears faded as did the pounding of my heart. Tara lay her head on my bare chest, gasping for breath.

"I'm afraid I interrupted you," I said between uneven breaths. "What were you saying about not joining me on my warbird?"

"Cocky Vandar." She swatted me on the chest. "No way are you getting rid of me now."

I grinned. "No?"

"Someone has to keep you in check," she said, kissing the mating marks on my chest.

I laughed. Things on my warbird were going to get interesting. But Kratos was right. I would never be bored.

I stroked her hair as I murmured one word over and over, loving the sound of it and savoring the fact that I could finally say it.

"Raisa, Raisa, Raisa."

She lifted her head. "I hope you're not saying another woman's name."

"There is no other woman," I said. "You are my Raisa. A Vandar Raas' true mate."

She brushed a kiss across my mating marks. "Yes, Raas."

EPILOGUE

Toraan

"Do you want to join your brothers in battle, Raas?"

I stood staring out the front of my warbird as first one Vandar horde, and then another, decloaked above Carlogia Prime. I'd intercepted the transmissions from Kaalek's *majak* and made a slight course adjustment to leave our sector, but now we remained invisible. Unseen and watching.

My command deck hummed with the crackle of incoming transmissions and the beeping of alerts. Thick boots rattled the iron floors as warriors changed shifts, but my gaze did not leave the battle stretched out before me.

I gripped my hands behind my back, carefully considering my answer and my strategy. "Negative." I strode to a nearby console, looking over the warrior's shoulder and reading the transmissions flying back and forth between the horde ships. "They have defeated the Zagrath on the planet's surface."

A murmur of approval spread through my command deck, although I knew my warriors would have preferred to be engaging in battle themselves, and not watching from afar. I would have enjoyed the thrill of battle as well, but the thought of seeing my brothers again—warriors I had not seen since I was a child—made my stomach roil.

I was not afraid of them. I was a Raas of the Vandar after all. I had been trained not to fear. But Kratos and Kaalek were strangers to me. The last time I had laid eyes on either of my elder brothers they'd been almost grown men, apprenticing on warbirds and uninterested in a younger brother who had been left behind with our mother on the Vandar settlement.

I moved one hand to the handle of my battle axe, the steel scales of armor covering one arm flexing with me. They would not even recognize me by now. Even though I shared their long black hair and dark eyes, I was as much of a stranger to them as they were to me. I knew more of our uncle, whose horde I'd apprenticed with, than I did of my own father. Considering my father's reputation, it was not something I regretted.

"Shall we retreat, Raas?" my *majak* asked.

"Retreat?" The word tasted bitter on my tongue. "When have we ever retreated?" I returned to my post in front of the ship's wide view into space. "We have the advantage of invisibility. Our fellow hordes have sacrificed that to engage in battle, but we remain hidden."

Serving under my uncle had taught me patience and strategy. He was not the most vicious Raas, but he had died the wealthiest and most powerful. The horde I inherited from him was vast, each ship richly outfitted and well-supplied with only the most advanced technology. My warriors were known, not only for their skill in battle, but for their cunning and shrewdness. When we attacked, we did not lose. I had too many warbirds and too many warriors to ever back down or ever suffer defeat.

"First, we outthink our enemy," my uncle had said, "then, we outfight them."

His philosophy had not been a traditionally Vandar one, which was probably why he and my father did not see eye to eye. But he had been the one to teach me and mold me, so it was his wisdom I carried.

I eyed the Zagrath battleship that had appeared above the planet. "Prepare a boarding party. While the empire is distracted by the battle with the other hordes and sending soldiers to fight on the surface, we can take the ship."

My *majak* clicked his heels sharply and turned to go. Then my eyes caught on something flying furtively away from the Zagrath ship. I reached for his arm to stay his departure.

"Wait. What is that?"

We both watched as a small shuttle flew underneath the battleship and then banked away from the planet.

"It is not joining the fight in the air or on the planet," my battle chief said, as he joined us.

I cocked my head. It looked very much like the shuttle was trying to leave under cover of battle. "Who on an imperial ship would want to escape during a battle with two Vandar hordes?"

"Someone who would risk their life to get away," my *majak* said.

The tips of my fingers tingled in anticipation. There was little I savored as much as a chase—or a mystery to unravel. I needed to know who was on that shuttle, and why they were running. Unless I was very wrong, a deserter would provide valuable intelligence about our enemy.

"Change of plans." I inclined my head at the small, gray vessel. "We're going to track that shuttle and take the pilot captive. Follow at a distance until we are clear from all Zagrath ships, then lock on and prepare a boarding party."

"Yes, Raas." My *majak* turned again, this time to go to his nearby standing console.

We moved unseen away from the planet and the volley of warring ships, and our departure seemed to go as unnoticed as the enemy shuttle's escape. "I'll be in my strategy room." I turned, and my battle kilt slapped the bare flesh of my legs. "Let me know when the pilot is on board."

I'd almost reached the door when my *majak* pivoted to face me. "Raas, our scans show that there is one life form aboard the shuttle."

"No surprise," I said, wondering why he'd made a point to tell me something we had expected.

"It is not a Zagrath," he continued.

That explained it. "A prisoner escaping?" My stomach tightened. "Is he Vandar?"

My *majak* shook his head, his gaze dropping. "No, Raas. A human. But it is not a 'he.' The life form on board the shuttle is a human female."

The tingles in my fingertips spread up my arms, my pulse thrummed, and my tail twitched. A female human? My gaze locked on the shuttle as we tracked it, and my hunting instincts fired.

Finally, prey worth hunting.

———

Thank you for reading PLUNDERED!

If you liked this alien barbarian romance, you'll love PILLAGED, book 3 in the series.

I was promised against my will to an imperial general. . . so I escaped. Right into the arms of an even more ruthless Vandar warlord.

One-click PILLAGED Now>

———

Want to get bonus scenes from all my books and be entered into fun giveaways? Join my VIP Reader group!

https://bit.ly/3lDzLOb

ALSO BY TANA STONE

Raider Warlords of the Vandar Series:

POSSESSED

PLUNDERED

PILLAGED

Alien Academy Series:

ROGUE (also available in AUDIO)

The Tribute Brides of the Drexian Warriors Series:

TAMED (also available in AUDIO)

SEIZED (also available in AUDIO)

EXPOSED (also available in AUDIO)

RANSOMED (also available in AUDIO)

FORBIDDEN (also available in AUDIO)

BOUND (also available in AUDIO)

JINGLED (A Holiday Novella)

CRAVED (also available in AUDIO)

STOLEN

SCARRED

The Barbarians of the Sand Planet Series:

BOUNTY (also available in AUDIO)

CAPTIVE (also available in AUDIO)

TORMENT (also available in AUDIO)

TRIBUTE

SAVAGE

CLAIM

TANA STONE books available as audiobooks!

ROGUE on AUDIBLE

BARBARIANS OF THE SAND PLANET

BOUNTY on AUDIBLE

CAPTIVE on AUDIBLE

TORMENT on AUDIBLE

TRIBUTE BRIDES OF THE DREXIAN WARRIORS

TAMED on AUDIBLE

SEIZED on AUDIBLE

EXPOSED on AUDIBLE

RANSOMED on AUDIBLE

FORBIDDEN on AUDIBLE

BOUND on AUDIBLE

CRAVED on AUDIBLE

ABOUT THE AUTHOR

Tana Stone is a bestselling sci-fi romance author who loves sexy aliens and independent heroines. Her favorite superhero is Thor (with Aquaman a close second because, well, Jason Momoa), her favorite dessert is key lime pie (okay, fine, *all* pie), and she loves Star Wars and Star Trek equally. She still laments the loss of *Firefly*.

She has one husband, two teenagers, and two neurotic cats. She sometimes wishes she could teleport to a holographic space station like the one in her tribute brides series (or maybe vacation at the oasis with the sand planet barbarians). :-)

She loves hearing from readers! Email her any questions or comments at tana@tanastone.com.

Want to hang out with Tana in her private Facebook group? Join on all the fun at: https://www.facebook.com/groups/tanastonestributes/

Printed in Great Britain
by Amazon